DEATH BY
TUMBLE DRYER

For Robert

Kelpies is an imprint of Floris Books
First published in 2017 by Floris Books
Text © 2017 David MacPhail. Illustrations © 2017 Floris Books

David MacPhail and Laura Aviñó have asserted their rights
under the Copyright, Designs and Patent Act 1988 to be
identified as the Author and Illustrator of this work

This publisher acknowledges subsidy from
Creative Scotland towards the publication of this volume

 Also available as an eBook

British Library CIP data available
ISBN 978-178250-426-9
Printed in Poland

DEATH BY TUMBLE DRYER

DAVID MACPHAIL
ILLUSTRATED BY LAURA AVIÑÓ

The Disappearing Dad

It was another cold, grey Glasgow day, with rain teeming down from the heavens. Everyone was sick of the weather. Even the seagulls looked depressed.

When I got home from school my hands were like blocks of ice, and my feet were soaking wet – although that wasn't from the rain, that was mainly down to Granny. She was lying across the carpet in the hall trying to bleed the radiators with a knitting needle. Water was scooshing everywhere, including over my shoes.

She jumped to her feet, like an ape that had just realised it was sitting on an ants' nest. "Out the way, ya balloon!" she yelled, barging me aside as she ran into the kitchen for a bucket. Her new project was 'doing up' the house, though it should really have been called 'undoing'. That was why the walls were full of holes, plaster was hanging off the ceiling and the boiler didn't work.

Granny was a tiny terrier of a woman, with thick glasses, wrinkles and long, grey hair. She always wore a green velour hoodie, along with matching jogging pants.

And when I say tiny I mean *tiny*. One Halloween she got

mistaken for Yoda from Star Wars, and she wasn't even dressed up.

Granny was busy mopping up the floor, and Mum wasn't back from work yet, so I thought I'd take the chance to do some long overdue detective work. I rolled up my sleeves and threw open the door of the large cupboard in Mum's bedroom. There was a lot of old stuff inside – all potential clues.

I gazed up at the top shelves, which were crammed with dusty boxes and plastic bags. I'd already rooted through them half a dozen times, but what if I'd missed something?

One thing.

A tiny clue.

Something to give the smallest hint why Dad disappeared.

This time I'd start at the very top. I'd reach as far back as I could. I stepped up onto the bottom shelf, bracing myself against the wall. And then a little higher still, testing the next shelf with my toe before stepping up onto it. I delved behind the front layer of boxes on the upmost shelf.

After a bit of stretching and groping my hand touched upon something. A thing right at the very back corner. A thing I hadn't found before. I wasn't sure why. Maybe I'd grown an inch since last time. It was a solid thing. A box of some sort. I strained some more, fingered it towards me then grabbed it with both hands.

An old shoebox. I took it to the bed and flipped off the lid. Inside, there was a stash of yellowing newspapers, letters and photos. Some of the photos were black and white, featuring the faces of long-lost relatives on the Indian side of the family. Grandad Sanjeev, my dad's dad, had died a few years ago. He left Delhi when he was eighteen and had never returned, except for the odd holiday. He loved it in Glasgow. He used to joke, "Where else can you go that has a monsoon twelve months of the year?"

Then I saw a pair of sunglasses poking out, and I knew it must be a box of his stuff. Grandad used to wear his sunglasses quite a lot, even at night, or in the dead of winter. I wasn't sure if it was a medical condition or if he was just trying to look cool. Anyhow, I was surprised he'd lived so long, as he was always walking into things. Glasgow gets quite dark in winter.

I flicked the sunglasses open and tried them on, tilting my head from side to side in the mirror. "Hmm, pretty cool."

Then I heard a cough – well, it was more like a bark, the bark of a small angry goblin. I turned to find Granny at the door. She was ogling me with a mix of horror and disgust, like I'd just vomited live snakes onto the carpet.

"Have you got nae respect for the dead?" she croaked, snatching the glasses away and then snapping the shoebox shut. She hurried off, chattering on about what I thought I was doing looking through poor Grandad's stuff. "Ya pure bahookie you are!"

I gazed back up at the shelves, then sighed and flopped

down on the bed. It had been nine months now. My eyes caught the tattered, yellowing poster on the wall, featuring my father wearing a turban, and staring down ominously at a crystal ball, surrounded by wisps of light.

It suddenly all felt pointless.

As pointless as a vanishing act where the magician actually vanishes, and doesn't come back? Yep, that pointless.

I closed my eyes, thinking about my life over the last few months – life with no father, a slightly unhinged granny and a completely unhinged mum – and wondering for the very first time if I should just give up searching for Dad and let him go. The police seemed to have stopped looking for him. Maybe they were right.

When I opened my eyes again, there was a face peering into mine. A strange face, a man's face, with smooth skin, a long nose and short grey hair. A man who was more than a bit familiar, except I was too busy jumping out of my skin to place him.

"AAAAGH!"

Then he opened his mouth and spoke, in a deep, disapproving voice – an Indian accent fused with Glaswegian.

"Have you been trying on my shades, boy?"

CHAPTER 2

The Greenish Grandad

"Who are you?" I blurted out to the face that had just appeared in front of mine.

"What do you mean, who am I?" he replied, insulted. "I am your grandfather."

I made a noise, which was a kind of half-groan, half-wail. I blinked my eyes open and shut, slapped myself on the cheeks, then stared at him again. He did look a bit like my grandad. And he certainly sounded like him. But it wasn't possible.

"Grandad's dead. He died years ago!"

He was wearing a thin, tweedy jacket and a brownish tie. Perched on top of his head was a silly sort of hat that he always wore, the kind of thing you see in black-and-white films. Grandad loved old American detective movies.

"Well, I am back now, am I not? Thanks to you." He wagged his finger in the direction of the dark glasses.

"Wait, what? Because I tried on your smelly old shades?"

He leaned closer. Now I could see that he was bathed in a sort of greenish glow. More worryingly, I could see the dresser through his face. He was actually transparent.

"Those are very special glasses, boy. Do not call them smelly."
He patted his jacket pocket. "Ach! I feel naked without them.
Would you believe it? The one time I leave the house without
my shades is the time I pop my clogs."

Up close, I could see the pores in his skin, and the thin
strands of hair brushed back over his ears. I darted into
the kitchen, edging past Granny, who was still jabbering.

I flung open the fridge door and checked the use-by date on the cheese, but it was fine.

"Well, if it's not food poisoning, then what is it?"

"Whit are you on aboot, eejit!" cried Granny.

I ran back into the bedroom, and the greenish apparition of my grandad was still there, fiddling with the cuffs of his jacket.

"I never much cared for this suit. I only wore it because your granny liked it. Look…" He turned to the forest of photos propped up on Granny's dresser. One faded picture was of him, Granny and my dad, who must have been only a few years older than me at the time. They were leaning over a rock jutting out into the sea, which was painted to look like a crocodile. Grandad was wearing the same suit he was wearing right now. "That was us at Millport, June 1987. Boy, life does not get any better than that day."

He turned his face to the door, and the sound of Granny's jabbering. "Ah, my girl! Where is she? I want to see her."

I followed him into the hall. He stood at the door of the kitchen, watching Granny hanging up her washing. She might have been a small woman but she had the most gigantic underwear you've ever seen. Her pants could have belonged to a rhinoceros. She was crooning some old song, sounding like a frog gargling on mouthwash:

"Cos ah gote me a real live kew-pee doll… and she's the cutest one of all."

Grandad folded his hands together under his chin. "Ah, there she is, still as beautiful as the day I left her." He opened out his arms towards her. "What do you say, my wee Scottish petal. Give me a big hug!"

"MUPPET!" Granny barked at me as she walked straight through him.

"OW!" cried Grandad as Granny scuttled out of the kitchen.

"She can't see you," I said.

"Clearly not." Grandad stared after her with a sappy grin. "I think only you can." Then he turned to me and opened out his arms. "Now, how about a hug for your grandfather."

"Alright," I grumbled and leant forward, only to find myself falling flat on my face into the recycling bin.

CRASH

Grandad stood over me, chortling. "A word of advice – never try to hug a ghost." He turned into the hall, before glancing back at me for a moment. "Oh, and never try on a dead man's shades."

The Jabbering Granny

In the living room, Granny was perched on one end of the sofa, where she always sat. She was knitting furiously and watching a game show on the TV, and getting annoyed at the contestants for getting their answers wrong.

Grandad sat at the other end, his hands clasped across his belly, just like he used to. It all seemed so natural, so normal, like he'd never been away. For a moment, I thought, perhaps he was real. Perhaps it wasn't my imagination, or that dodgy egg I had for breakfast. Perhaps it really *was* him back from the dead. I suddenly found my voice cracking, my eyes welling up with tears.

"Grandad, is it *really* you?"

But Grandad wasn't listening. He thrust out his hand towards the TV and bellowed, "What is this rubbish you are watching, woman?" He turned his face to me and grunted. "I HATE quiz shows. I mean, what about a programme about flying doctors, or a documentary about sharks?"

"WHIT?" cried Granny, cupping her hand to her ear. She was a bit hard of hearing. Then she turned back to the telly and went on jabbering at it.

"I don't understand," I said to Grandad. "I mean... why?"

"Why have I returned?" he asked. "Well, I am not sure yet."

He scratched his head. He seemed confused for a moment, before standing up and swiping his hand at the TV. "Ach, I cannot watch this. If only I could use the what-do-you-call-it."

The what-do-you-call-it was the name he gave the remote control. He beckoned me out of the room with him. "Come on."

Outside in the hall, he pointed at the holes in the walls. "Your granny did this?"

"She's 'fixing up' the house," I said.

Grandad shook his head wistfully. "What a woman! She always was a good fixer-upper."

We went into my room, which looked like someone had first burgled it, then ransacked it, then finally turned it upside down and shaken it violently. It was my operations centre. Piles of Dad's papers and batches of newspaper cuttings clogged up the desk and the floor. A large map of the Glasgow area was pinned across one wall beside a corkboard covered with notes, Post-its and photos, all connected up with orange string in a sort of web.

"So you all live here now?" he asked.

I nodded. Me and Mum moved in with Granny after Dad disappeared.

Grandad gazed around and whistled. "Jayesh, what is the idea with the mess here?"

"I wasn't exactly expecting visitors."

He shuffled awkwardly and fiddled with his collar. "Anyway, so, eh... how are you, boy? Are you good?"

"Well... no." I slumped down on the bed, trying to find a way of explaining the twists and turns my life had taken over the last year.

Grandad caught sight of himself in the mirror. He gazed closely at his reflection, before screwing up his face. He stuck his hands in his pockets, suddenly looking sad and forlorn.

"Um... What about you?" I asked.

He puffed out his cheeks. "Oh, you know, dead." He glanced at his reflection again, before shivering. "I think." He waved his hands at the corkboard. "So what is all this? The strings."

Before I could explain, the house phone started to ring. I went into the hall and checked the caller ID.

It was Mum's mobile number. I held my finger up at Grandad. "Hold on. This isn't over."

I picked it up, expecting to hear Mum, but it wasn't her. It sounded like clothes sloshing around inside a washing machine. Then I realised it was actually someone's mouth with chewing gum swirling round inside it.

"Hullo, Jay?" A flat, monotone voice.

"Hullo, yes?"

"It's Mrs McCleary, from the school." Mum worked part-time in the library at my school, and Mrs McCleary was her boss. I could hear angry shouting in the background, and a lot of thumping. "Listen, son, you better get up here."

"Why?" I asked. "What's wrong?"

"Your mammy, she's flipped. The police are here."

"Flipped? The police?"

"Aye son. Flipped."

"I'll be right there," I said, and hung up.

"What is it, boy?" asked Grandad.

"I'm not sure, but I think Mum is being arrested."

CHAPTER 4

The Speedy Woman

I explained to Granny why I needed to get to school – sharpish.

"Oh, GEE-MIGHTY FATHER!" She flapped around like a tiny, panicking bird and snatched the car keys out of the bowl, while I grabbed my parka coat.

Our transport was a battered old VW campervan, which Mum had painted lime green. The interior was decked out in rich Indian fabrics, with stringy beads hanging down over the windscreen.

"What a heap of junk you are driving," said Grandad. "Where is your father? He needs a talking to."

I shook my head. "He's gone, Grandad."

"What? Gone?"

"WHIT?" yelped Granny as she jumped in the driver's seat.

I opened the passenger door and was about to get in.

"Wait," said Grandad. "What about me?

I shrugged. "What about you?"

"You must open the door for your grandfather, Jayesh Patel."

I closed my door over a bit, shielding my conversation

from Granny. She was busy in any case, adjusting the seat and mirrors to Yoda-level. "You're transparent. Can't you just float through it?"

"Haayy! No, boy, I am not doing that." He shivered like he'd just seen a ghost, except *he* was the ghost.

I sighed, shook my head and slid open the back door for him, watching him flit past me into the back seat. "Thank you, boy."

What kind of a ghost was he, I thought, that he couldn't even go through things? I was beginning to remember how annoying Grandad could be at times.

Granny squawked at me. "Come OAN, ya puddin'!"

I got in, fastened my safety belt then assumed the crash position. Granny only ever drove in an emergency, and for good reason. Usually it was *her* causing the emergency.

"What do you mean, your father's gone?" asked Grandad.

"Gone," I said, with my head lodged between my legs. "Disappeared about nine months ago. We still don't know what happened to him."

"Whit? Whit, whit?" yapped Granny.

Grandad leaned forward, his face creasing with worry. "Disappeared, you say? That does not sound like him."

Granny was hunched over the steering wheel, her face practically pressed up against the windscreen. Beads of sweat were trickling down her forehead. She hated driving. She was shrieking at a pedestrian, swiping her hand at the man to get out of her way – even though he was on a zebra crossing and *she* was supposed to stop for him.

Fortunately, the man looked up at the last moment. His jaw dropped in terror, then he dived aside, goalie-style as she zoomed through.

While Granny was distracted I told Grandad about Dad. How he disappeared in the middle of his great 'vanishing act'. This was a stage routine he did where he seemed to disappear into a box, but then reappear from the wings. Except this time, he didn't reappear. He vanished off the face of the Earth and was never seen again. "It made front-page news and everything," I said.

He nodded. "Ah, now that *does* sound like your father." Then he rubbed his chin. "Jayesh, I am sorry, but as a magician your father was... uh..."

"Rubbish? I know."

Grandad sniggered. "Do you remember the time he did that act where he pulled the white dove out of the hat?"

"Yeah," Now I sniggered too. Dad kept the dove hidden under his shirt, so he could switch it into his top hat at the last moment. Except this time the dove got free, and started flapping about like crazy underneath the shirt.

We both burst out laughing. "He was thrashing around like a madman," said Grandad, "shrieking, trying to catch it."

I nodded. "The feathers were flying everywhere, out of his collar, his sleeves. To be fair, the audience loved it."

"They thought he was a comedian, not a magician," added Grandad. Then, after a moment, he added, "But where can he have got to?"

"Grandad," I said, after a pause, "you're a ghost. Can't you see things we can't?"

"Well, I tell you one thing," He pointed to the sky. "He is not up there. I would have seen him if he was."

I felt a spark of hope. If he wasn't 'up there', that meant he was still down here... somewhere. Then I remembered I was talking to an illusion, an image I was seeing of my dead grandfather. If it wasn't food poisoning, or some kind of gas, I don't know – I was probably just dreaming the whole thing. Maybe in a minute I would wake up, having nodded off on the couch.

Grandad looked at me through narrowed eyes. "Hmm... so that is what you have been doing, with all the string and the maps and papers. You are trying to find him."

"The police stopped looking," I said. "So I started doing it myself."

Grandad scratched his forehead. "Oh dear, I am sorry, boy. Have you found any clues?"

"I've gone through everything – all his papers, his e-mails, his phone messages. I've spoken to everyone who knew him... The only thing I have to show for it is this."

I unzipped a pocket on the arm of my parka and pulled out a small rectangular stub – a subway ticket.

Grandad tried to take it between his pinched fingers, but they just went through it. He tutted. "Oho! I cannot get used to this 'being a ghost' business at all."

"I found this in his dressing room after the magic show.

It was the only thing he left behind." The ticket was for a station called St Enoch at one minute past twelve on the day he disappeared.

I flipped it over to show him the writing on the back. "It's a name I think."

It was scrawled in blue ink in my Dad's own hand. "I've never been able to find out who he was, or how my Dad knew him. That's if it *is* a name. Maybe it's not a man at all. Maybe it's a company, or a place name. Who knows?"

Grandad stared at it for a while, shaking his head.

He groaned. "Haayy! All I know is that I am back here for a purpose. I wonder if it is to help you find your father?"

The school appeared on the left. My stomach lurched as Granny swung the car off the road and mounted the kerb.

"Come OAN!" she croaked, jumping out of the car and racing around the front, before leaping up the school steps two at a time.

"Ahh!" said Grandad warmly. "She is just as speedy as the day I married her. Never underestimate a speedy woman."

I rolled my eyes as I got out. "I'll remember that."

CHAPTER 5

The Fierce Stooshie

I burst into the school library behind Granny, to find Mum at the centre of a fight. No, correction: she *was* the fight. Katie Patel was wearing a long, flowery dress and a pair of burgundy Dr. Martens. Mum called herself an 'innocent child of nature', but that's not how she looked right now, with her face scrunched up into a snarl and a man in a headlock. Judging by the suit the man was wearing, his freckles and sandy hair, I took it to be Mr Kessock, our head teacher.

Mum was yelling, nostrils flaring:

"How DARE you! How DARE you! Calling me a liar!"

Mr Kessock was shrieking in his panicky nasal voice:

"Help! Someone help me! She's got my head!"

The school secretary, Mrs Cravat, was a prim lady with blonde hair tied in a bun, a black-and-white twin-set and a beaded necklace. She was half-heartedly trying to wrest Mr Kessock's head free. "Oh, do let him go!"

There were also two police officers in the fray. One of them was a plain-clothes detective. From the investigations into Dad's disappearance, I'd come to recognise the sort: grim-faced to the point of serious illness, and wearing a cheap navy suit. This one was a woman. She was trying to separate everyone, without much success. "Release that man, madam, and MOVE AWAY!"

The other policeman was in uniform. He was dancing about like a boxer, his truncheon raised and a look of relish on his face. "Can I hit them, Boss? Oh, go on! Can I?"

Mum's boss, Mrs McCleary, was sitting behind a desk with her feet up, chewing gum and watching the kerfuffle unfold. She was enjoying herself, nodding and applauding. "This is brilliant!"

Now Granny got in on the action. She may have been little but she was fierce. She leapt onto the detective's back, with an ear-splitting war cry:

"STOOSHIE!"

"Aaargh!" The detective swung round and round, trying to throw her off. "What!? Get off me!"

"WHEEEE!" cried Granny.

"The world has gone mad since I left," said Grandad.

Fortunately, I had a plan. Mum's bag was lying open behind the counter. I delved inside and fished out her panic alarm.

HHHHONNNNKKKKKKK!

Everyone stopped. The detective froze with Granny still on her back. Mum blinked around the room as if emerging from a trance. She let Mr Kessock go, beamed and stretched out her arms toward me: "Dearie!"

Mr Kessock reeled back, choking and clutching his throat.

"Uch, don't be such a drama queen," joked Mrs McCleary.

Mrs Cravat rubbed his back. "Are you alright, Mr Kessock?"

The head teacher steadied himself against a bookcase, screwed up his face to a weasly scowl and pointed an accusing finger at Mum. "That woman... ASSAULTED me! She needs to be sacked."

Mrs McCleary had by this time picked up a magazine, and was flipping through it. "No way! I'm the boss in this library, not you. Besides, this is the best entertainment I've had in weeks." She turned and gave me a wink, before licking her index finger and flicking a few pages.

"What!?" croaked Mr Kessock. "You're taking her side?"

He gave a slack-jawed look of appeal to the detective, pointing his finger now at Mrs McCleary. "She's got it in for me as well. I'm up for Head Teacher of the Year, you know." He smoothed his wispy ginger hair and screwed up his face even more, if that was even possible. "She hates that."

"Mrs Patel is a wee bit emotional, detective," replied Mrs McCleary. "Her husband disappeared, remember?"

"What's going on?" I asked, even though I wasn't sure I wanted to know.

Granny sprang to the ground like a mad frog. The detective turned and ogled her, then looked embarrassed as she realised she'd just been jumped by a tiny old lady. She straightened her jacket, then turned and ogled me instead. "Who are you two?"

"Want me to frisk them, Boss?" said the constable, swinging his truncheon about. "That old lady attacked you, and that wee boy looks like a troublemaker if I ever saw one."

Mum thrust an accusing finger right back at Mr Kessock. "He called me a liar."

Mr Kessock's voice was hoarse with annoyance. "There is NO body!"

"A body?" I said. "What body?"

"It's OK, there is no body," said the detective, exasperated.

"There *was* a body," replied Mum. "Right here." She jabbed her finger at a spot on the floor.

"She's demented!" cried Mrs Cravat.

"She ASSAULTED me!" repeated Mr Kessock.

"WHIT?! WHIT?!" snapped Granny, staring from one face to the other.

"Shall I handcuff her, Boss?" asked the constable. "Ah, go on! Can I?"

Grandad laughed out loud. "The world really has gone mad!"

Mum pointed to a spot on the floor right in front of where she was standing. "A dead body, it was right here, I'm telling you."

"A dead body?" I asked. "In the school library?"

CHAPTER 6

The Invisible Body

I gazed at the spot on the floor where Mum was pointing. There were no clues, no strange marks, no suspicious bloodstains. It was just an ordinary bit of an ordinary floor in an ordinary school library.

"I saw him, I touched him. I took his pulse," said Mum. She turned to the detective. "I even described him to you."

"Yes." The detective flipped open her notebook and read from it. "You said you came into the library alone, to find a man of about five foot eleven, with ginger hair, a goatee beard, and a brown suit with a navy-blue shirt and tie lying on the floor."

"Yes," said Mum.

"You found him not to be breathing. Whereupon you screamed and ran into the office next door." The detective turned to Mrs Cravat. "And then *you* called the police." Mrs Cravat nodded. The detective looked round at Mrs McCleary and Mr Kessock. "While the rest of you all rushed back in here, where you found the alleged body to be gone."

"Alleged?" snapped Mr Kessock in his whiny voice. "Non-existent! She's making it up!"

The detective raised her hand firmly then continued. "How long were you out of the room in total?"

"A minute at most," said Mum.

The detective shrugged her shoulders and flipped her notebook closed. "So where could a dead body have gone in the space of a minute? We've searched the building, haven't we, Constable?"

She glanced at the constable, who huffed. "Yeah, and we found nothing. I'd flippin' love to see a dead body."

The detective grasped Mum by the elbows. "We found nothing, do you hear? Now, are you sure you're feeling well today? Have you forgotten to take any important medication?"

"No!" said Mum.

The detective eyed her up and down, taking in the eccentric way Mum was dressed. She raised an eyebrow. "Are you quite sure?"

Mum scowled. "Quite sure? I am totally positive."

There was a burst of static from the detective's radio, and a muffled voice came over it. She turned away to exchange a few words with the controller on the other end, before turning back and signalling to the constable. "We have to go."

The constable's shoulder's drooped. "Uch! I was hoping for a right good rammy there." He turned to me, explaining, "This is my first week in the job, and there hasn't been much action."

"Well, we have an actual police incident to attend to now,

not an imaginary one. The seagulls are shoplifting from the newsagents again. Come on." She stopped beside me on her way out the door, and whispered, "Are you her carer, son?"

Grandad burst out laughing. "Oh-ho-ho, that is a good one."

"Eh, kind of," I said. It wasn't far from being the truth.

"He is my son," called Mum from the other side of the room.

"She's my mum," I said.

"Look, you seem like the most sensible one in your family," said the detective. "Your mum's lucky I'm not charging her for wasting police time." She turned and eyed Granny again. "As for that old lady – who's she, your granny?"

I nodded.

She looked at me with what could only be described as pity. "She's lucky, too, I could have charged *her* for attacking a police officer." She leant closer still and raised a finger at me. "My name is Detective Inspector Dawn Graves, and I do not want to hear from your family again. Please try to keep them under control. Is that clear?"

The police left, while Mr Kessock stormed off into the office next door, followed by his secretary.

"Bravo! That was absolutely brilliant!" Mrs McCleary closed her magazine and stood up. "How could you fail to see the funny side of Mr Kessock getting a doing? Now, let's all have a cup of tea to celebrate."

She put the kettle on, and Mum and Granny went to help. While everyone was distracted I pushed through the door of the library and headed off down the corridor.

"Hey!" It was Grandad's voice, following behind me. "Slow down, will you?"

"You're a ghost!" I said. "Can't you just float quicker?"

"Do not disrespect me, boy," he said. "I may be a ghost, but I am still your grandfather. Now where are you going?"

"To find out if Mum's right."

CHAPTER 7

The Carpeted Corpse

Mum had imagined quite a lot of things in her time: fairy paths, ley lines, even leprechauns. But she'd never imagined anything as realistic as a dead body. It just wasn't her thing. And if there really was a corpse, how could it just disappear in a matter of seconds?

Big Davie was the school caretaker. I found him at his desk, which was in a cluttered office in the school basement. He was attacking the inner workings of a printer with a big screwdriver.

As soon as he clocked a school uniform walking through the door he panicked. "Children! Out!" He held up a small bottle of disinfectant and sprayed it frantically in my direction. "OUT!"

"Hm, what is the idea with this guy?" said Grandad.

"He hates children," I said. "Thinks they carry disease."

"OUT, I said!"

Grandad chortled. "Haaay! He is working in the wrong place!"

I held up my palms to show I meant no harm. "Davie, it's only me."

"Patel?" He glanced at his watch. "Here, school finished over an hour ago. Why are you still here?"

"I did go home, Davie, but I had to come back." I explained what happened with Mum.

"I see." He nodded. "Well, I'd be at home the now as well, except the music department's moving buildings, so I've to oversee the shifting of Mrs Murray's grand piano. They're lifting it through the window by a winch in half an hour."

I propped myself on the edge of his desk, the one bit that wasn't taken up with tins of paint or bits of machinery.

"OFF, OFF, OFF!" he cried, aiming his bottle of disinfectant at me.

"Davie, I've got a favour to ask you. Can I check the school CCTV for the west exit?"

"Clever boy," said Grandad. "Here, should the police not be doing that? I mean, what do we pay our taxes for anyway?"

"You don't pay taxes," I said, "you're dead."

Davie looked at me quizzically for a second before saying, "The answer's no," and shooing me off. "Don't come too close, I told you before. Don't come within one metre." He held up his thumb and forefinger in front of his face. "See that? That's how far a tiny miniature virus can travel on average. And children are full of tiny miniature viruses."

"This guy is one crate short of a lorryload," said Grandad, before leaning forward. "That is an old cash-and-carry joke." Grandad used to run a cash-and-carry business when he was alive. No, he never made it as a professional comedian.

I picked up a piece of the printer Davie had been working on and toyed with it, making sure I smudged my fingerprints all over it. I did this just to annoy him. "Davie, have you forgotten you owe me a favour?"

He snatched it off me. "What favour?"

"Like when I helped you track down the bike thief, or when I discovered who was spraying graffiti on the bike sheds, or..."

"Aye, OK, OK," he cut in. "You can check." Davie ushered me over to a bank of old-fashioned dusty screens. "I rarely look at them myself." He tapped the screen on the bottom left. "This is the one you're looking for." He showed me how to rewind and play, then he left, doing a sort of chirping whistle that he always did.

"Weird man, your jannie," said Grandad. "Now what do you see?"

It didn't take me long to find him: the man with the ginger hair, goatee beard and brown suit. He entered the building about fifteen minutes before Mum said she saw him lying dead on the floor of the library.

Grandad gasped. "So she was right, eh? Well, it looks like we have got a mystery on our hands."

I forwarded the recording ten minutes. "If you're a ghost," I said, as it wound on, "can you not see other ghosts? As in, the recently deceased? As in, the ghost of the man from the library?"

Grandad shrugged. "Not always. Most people go straight on up. Only a few hang about or come back down, like me."

"Well, that's about as helpful as a slap in the face," I said. About eight minutes passed on the video, and a van reversed into the corner of the picture. I couldn't see much, just a logo on the side. I paused it, and gazed closer. I could just make out the wording:

Duke's Laundry
Govanhill

Two men got out. One was short and fat, the other was tall and thin. They wore white overalls and masks, the kind of thing you see crime-scene investigation people wearing. Strangely, though, they were wearing beanie hats, which are definitely *not* the kind of thing you see crime-scene investigation people wearing.

The two men entered the building, then I forwarded the recording to the fifteen-minute mark and let it play. A moment later they reappeared, carrying between them what looked like a rolled-up carpet.

"Look!" I said, as they bundled the carpet into the van.

"What?" said Grandad, unable to see anything.

"Oh, aye!" It was Davie this time, who'd come back in.

"What?" said Grandad. I can't see it.

"Wait, I'll rewind ten seconds," I said.

"Aye, go back," said Davie.

I rewound a bit and let it play again.

"Now freeze," I said. I hit pause, just as the two men turned slightly, pointing the end of the carpet towards the camera.

"Yup, right there," said Davie.

"You still can't see it?" I said to Grandad.

Davie traced his finger along the screen in a tiny curve.

"Yes, of course I can!" Only now did Grandad see it. Or rather – *them*.

A pair of feet, wearing brown brogues, jutting out the end of the carpet.

"Yup, we've got a corpse," I said.

CHAPTER 8

The Unwanted Guest

We sat gazing in shock at the school's CCTV screen as the van drew away.

"I am back one hour," said Grandad. "First I find that my son is missing and now someone is dead. What is the world coming to?"

Davie's face was chalk white. "What if it's contagious?"

"We'd better phone the police," I said.

Davie shook his head. "Not you, son, I'll do it."

"He is right Jayesh," said Grandad. "Let an adult do it."

I nodded, thinking about what that DI Graves said to me. She made it pretty clear she didn't want to hear from my family again.

"Well," Davie looked at his watch, "after I've finished shifting that grand piano, I'll phone from the school office."

I was fine with that. I didn't want to draw any attention to myself. I could prove that my mum was right, but the police would never know the evidence had come from me.

Davie flapped his hands. "Now, you skidaddle! You're filling up my office with germs."

"Ha!" said Grandad. "If only he knew there was a ghost in here as well."

"You can take the credit for it, Davie," I said as we pushed the door open. "Don't mention I was here."

"Are you going to tell your mother?" asked Grandad as we made our way back to the library.

"No, let her find out from the police." One thing I'd noticed from reading detective stories was that the best detectives were invisible. No one paid them any attention. No one accounted for them. And quite often nobody knew it was them who was sniffing around, about to crack the case. Most importantly, the person who had committed the crime never knew.

"Jayesh, the boy detective," chuckled Grandad.

I shrugged, but it was kind of true. I *was* a detective. I had to be. How else was I going to track down my Dad?

When we got back to the library Mum and Granny were just finishing their cups of tea.

"Where have you been?" croaked Granny.

I shrugged. "Toilet."

The four of us – me, Mum, Granny and the ghost of my dead grandad – got into the campervan. Grandad floated into the back with me. Mum drove this time. Unfortunately a car journey with her was no less relaxing than a car journey with Granny. She spent half of it practising her 'mindfulness' deep-breathing exercises and the other half snarling at other drivers. A man in a black taxi cut her up at a junction. As she opened her mouth and shouted, all her floaty mindfulness melted away and out came the rabid Glaswegian underneath. "What do you think you're doing, you bleeping muppet!?" Although she didn't really say 'bleeping'.

Then Granny made us stop by B&Q so she could buy a new hammer drill. She was so eager she unboxed it before we even got through the checkout. Her eyes lit up with delight and her tongue poked out the side of her mouth as she gazed it over.

Grandad clasped his hands together and stared at her wistfully. "Ah, I love it when she gets that determined look."

She walked out with it slung over her shoulder like a heavy machine gun. With her hood up, she looked like a gangland assassin. I've never seen people scatter so fast.

Back home at last, Mum set about making dinner. Granny couldn't wait to put her drill to use. She started drilling holes in the wall before she'd even taken her coat off. As for me, I went to the loo, or at least I tried to, but Grandad followed me in.

"What are you doing?" I said.

He glanced around as if he didn't quite know what I was bothered about. "Haunting you?" he said.

"I'm going to the toilet."

He stared at me for a second, as if he'd forgotten that going to the toilet was a private thing. Then he nodded and turned away.

Finally we sat down to dinner. It had been a long day, and only now did I realise how hungry I was.

"What's for tea?" asked Grandad, rubbing his hands.

"What do you care? You can't eat," I replied.

"WHIT?" said Granny.

"Oh, I forgot." Grandad looked sadly down at his see-through stomach.

Mum whipped her latest culinary creation out of the oven. "Ta-daaaa!" She hoofed the oven door shut behind her. "Seaweed and quinoa pie."

To say I was disappointed was an understatement. It looked and smelt like something a mermaid had vomited onto the rocks.

"It's organic," she declared, as if that was an excuse.

Grandad sighed and shook his head. "Hayyy! I am so sorry, boy." It was like he was telling me someone had died. "To think of all the lovely food your father and I used to cook for you."

But all was not lost. Granny snuck her hand under the table and pulled out a chip. Somehow, she'd managed to sneak out the flat and down to *Luigi's* to pick up a fish supper.

She winked at me and passed me a chip.

Grandad tried to snatch one too, but he passed right through it. "Ach!" he wailed. "I hate being a ghost."

All evening, I kept waiting for the phone to go, or the doorbell to ring, and for those two grumpy police officers to appear looking sheepish and apologetic, but they never did.

"Maybe they'll call your mum in for questioning tomorrow," said Grandad.

This was serious business. Someone had died at our school – probably been murdered. Would the police really just leave it until tomorrow? The more time passed, the more it bothered me.

And Grandad bothered me too. Surely, if seeing him was down to some weird food poisoning, the effects would have worn off by now. But as the night drew on he was still there, hogging the sofa and shouting at the television.

Just supposing, I thought, he really was my grandad returned from the grave. Did I really want him to go away?

"Why?" I asked him, as I was in my room getting ready for bed. "Why are you here?"

"I don't really know, Jayesh. Maybe there is no reason. Can you not just accept that your old grandfather is back?"

I sighed. "I give up. I'm going to bed." I turned down my bed covers.

"And what am I supposed to do while you are asleep?" he asked indignantly.

"I don't know. Can't you go and haunt someone else?"

"I am serious. Ghosts cannot sleep. I also cannot pick things up or touch anything. Which means I cannot flick through a magazine or a book, and I cannot change the channels on the television."

I groaned. "I don't suppose I'm ever going to get any sleep with you mooching about." I took him back into the lounge. Mum and Granny had already gone to bed. I stuck the TV on for him. "There you go."

"Wait, what is this?" It was some home DIY show, presented by a pair of grinning men wearing utility belts.

"It's the only thing on," I said. "Unless you want to watch a programme about badgers?"

"No, no, that won't do. There must be something else to watch. What about *Miami Vice*? Or *The Bill*, do you still get that?"

I shrugged my shoulders. "Never heard of it."

"It was the best TV programme ever made. This is rubbish."

"I'm sorry, this really is the best thing on." I made to go, but he called me back.

"Wait, wait, wait. It's so quiet, I can't hear it. Put the subtitles on for me, will you?"

I groaned, and snatched the remote. I couldn't quite believe I was putting on subtitles for my hard-of-hearing ghost grandad. "Right, I'm off, goodnight."

I switched the light out. Even though he was my grandad, I half-hoped that by tomorrow he'd be gone.

He wasn't.

In fact, I came into the living room to find him inspecting our artex ceiling. "Who did you get to do the roof, boy? It is a disgrace. Cowboy builders, I bet." He'd been watching back-to-back DIY shows all night and now all of a sudden he was an expert.

Just then, Mum came hurtling into the room, holding her phone. "Oh, Jay, Jay! Did you hear what happened to Big Davie?"

That hit me like a brick wall. Alarm bells rang and hairs stood on the back of my neck. "What?"

"Big Davie, the caretaker from the school."

I don't know whether it was a good guess, or whether seeing ghosts had given me the power of second sight, but I couldn't help blurting out, "He's dead."

And I was right.

CHAPTER 9

The Squashed Jannie

"Don't tell me," I said, before the shock had even set in. "He was squashed to death by a grand piano." My stomach churned at the thought.

Mum gave me a funny look. "How did you know?"

"Yes," said Grandad. "How did you know?"

I shrugged. "Lucky guess."

Davie had said he was on his way to shift the piano before going to the office to call the police, so it was the first thing that entered my mind. I could just imagine it: a giant crane winching the grand piano out of the window, him standing underneath motioning it forward, and...

Then another thought struck me. What if someone found out he knew something? What if that someone didn't want the police to know? What if – SNAP – someone with the means and the motive to cause an accident sent the piano crashing down on top of him? Maybe I had a suspicious mind. Or maybe I was onto something. "Poor Davie," I said.

I was so stunned I could have fallen over, except I was already sitting down. Mum rushed towards me, tears in her eyes, and wrapped her arms around me. Unfortunately, she had to go through Grandad on the way.

"OUCH!" he cried.

"I'll light a candle for him in my shrine of remembrance," she said. This might sound quite touching, but bear in mind her 'shrine of remembrance' was the top of the toilet cistern.

Granny wandered in, dressed in a kind of brown tunic, which was covered in dust and plaster. I soon realised it was her old Brownies uniform. It fit her again after all these years. No wonder; she seemed to be shrinking. She was muttering under her breath, "A pian-a! A pian-a! People should be more careful!"

"That's one missing son and TWO people dead, and I've not even been here twenty-four hours," said Grandad, as Mum wandered out of the living room. "At least this one was an accident."

"Accident? ACCIDENT?" I said.

"You think it was not an accident?" Grandad echoed.

"PAH!" spat Granny, wielding her new hammer drill like a heavy machine gun. "Accidents! Health and safety is for wimps!" She stormed out like a character from a war film, charging straight through Grandad in the process.

"Ow-eeeee!"

I told Grandad about my theory: that if someone found out what Davie knew, they might have wanted to stop him telling the police. Grandad rubbed his non-existent chin, while I grabbed my schoolbag. "I'm going to check it out."

I passed Mum and Granny on the way out the door. They were both in the loo. Mum was kneeling in front of the shrine on top of the toilet, raising her hands in the air, shaking them about and chanting. Granny, meanwhile, was struggling to control a giant spurt from one of the taps.

"A leak! I've got a leak!"

"Have a nice day!" I grabbed my parka and left the chaos behind me.

"Hey!" Grandad called out, as I vaulted down the stairs and into the street. "Hey! Wait! Wait on me!"

I stopped. "Grandad, I'm going to school."

"You said you were going to check out what happened to your jannie. I want to come too," he said.

"You can't come to school with me."

"Why not?"

I argued with him for a while, but it was no use. He was determined to come. Besides, the people at the bus stop were starting to give me weird looks.

"Does this mean you go everywhere with me now?" I asked as I hurried along.

"Well, I am haunting you, you know," he replied. "Now slow down a bit. I am not as fit as I once was."

"You're not even remotely fit," I said. "You're dead!"

"Oh, rub it in, why don't you?" He patted his breast pocket, which was empty, not to mention being transparent, and sighed. "Wish I had my sunglasses."

Grandad acted very strangely as we were walking up the street. He kept shifting from my left side to my right, then back again, and shielding his eyes, muttering "Haay! Haaaayy!" I couldn't work out what he was doing. I thought he was having some kind of spectral breakdown. But I was more concerned with getting to school in good time, so that I could snoop around. Unfortunately, Grandad's ghost was barely faster now than when he was alive and geriatric.

"Surely a ghost can move quicker than that?" I said.

"Do not disrespect me, boy!" he replied. "I am just getting used to floating, that is all."

So, by the time we got to school the bell was about to go. Which meant I had barely enough time to check anything out. All I could do was pay a quick visit to the scene of the 'accident'.

The car park behind the music department was sealed off. An area was surrounded by tape and a blue police tent had been set up around the remains of the grand piano. The crane was still there.

"To think he was worried about germs," said Grandad.

The bell rang, but I could barely think about my lessons. I had bigger things on my mind, like who was the killer in my school?

CHAPTER 10

The Invisible Sidekick

"I've got to get to class," I told Grandad.

"I will come with you," he said.

"No, you can't."

"Why not?"

I sighed. I always imagined being haunted would be quite scary, or at least interesting, but actually I was finding it really annoying. "Haven't you got anything better to do?"

He looked down at himself and opened out his arms. "As it happens, no."

"Why don't you go home?" I said. "Have a nice sit down on the settee and wait for me to come back from school."

"There is nothing to do at home except yell at your granny, and she cannot even hear me."

"Go for a walk, then," I said. "Oh, sorry, I mean a float. You could do with the practice."

He looked offended, and then a bit frightened. "On my own? It is scary out there."

"You're a flippin' ghost, Grandad. What have *you* got to be scared of?"

"Other ghosts," he replied. "And some of them are real belters. They are everywhere. On the streets, peering out of windows. And they look how they did when they died, so some have big gashes in their heads, some have limbs hanging off. You can't see them, but I can."

Only now did I remember the strange way he'd been acting on the way to school. Now I realised, he was shying away from his fellow spooks.

"So," I summarised, "the main reason you want to follow me around is you're scared of ghosts, even though you're one yourself?"

"That is about the long and the short of it," he replied. "So let us go to class."

In spite of my best efforts, Grandad trailed after me into my classroom. I sat down at my desk, while Grandad propped himself up against the doorframe watching the teacher, Mrs Murray.

"We're going to start with geography," she said. She yanked down a large world map from the blackboard, then stuck her pointer at South America. "Now, Argentina…"

Grandad gave a huge theatrical yawn. "Ugh… geography. Yawnamundo."

I glared at him. "Shhh!" This got me funny looks, not only from my classmates, but also from Mrs Murray. I had to think fast to cover my tracks. "Shhh… shhh… shhilver. Eh, the name Argentina comes from the Latin word for silver: *argentum*."

"Very good, Jayesh," said the teacher.

Grandad grinned and pointed his two forefingers at me. "NIIICE!"

"Swot!" sniped Anton, the boy who sat in front of me and was probably my worst enemy in the world – apart from my Mum's cooking.

I sunk my head into my hands. The school day was going to be torture.

At breaktime, I decided to hang out with Pyotr. He was one of my best pals. At least, I think he was. Pyotr didn't talk much. Mainly because he had only just moved here from Poland and was still learning English. We hung out a lot, usually watching Epic Fail videos on YouTube. He also had this crazy, infectious laugh, like a braying donkey, but not quite as annoying as an actual braying donkey might be.

The great thing about hanging out with Pyotr was that it meant I could speak to Grandad. Pyotr couldn't understand what I was saying, so he had no idea I was talking to a ghost. Meanwhile everyone else thought I was just talking to Pyotr, so it didn't look like I'd lost my mind and was talking to someone who wasn't there.

We leant over Pyotr's tablet, watching videos, with Grandad at my shoulder.

"We need to check out the jannie's office," I said to Grandad out the side of my mouth.

"What for?" he asked.

"The CCTV recording. That's our evidence. We need it."

Pyotr helpfully nodded along, until some kid on YouTube fell off a rope swing and plunged into a river, at which point he erupted into one of his crazy laughs.

Mwa-hawhaw-heehe!!

I joined in, just for appearances' sake, then I turned back to Grandad. "Not now, though. We'll go at lunchtime."

"I don't understand," said Grandad. "Why not now?"

"Because the jannie's office will be quiet at lunchtime." I'd heard there was a stand-in janitor. I didn't know him, I didn't know when he was likely not to be there. But I *did* know that lunch was peak time for cleaning up vomit, breaking up fights and responding to hoax fire alarms.

By the time lunch came, Grandad was well on the way to screwing up my education. We'd done English, maths and drama, and he'd declared all of them equally 'yawnamundo'. It was difficult to concentrate on anything. He kept making stupid comments, or talking over the teacher, or looking over my shoulder when I was working and then sucking air sharply through his teeth when he read my answers.

Not to mention my social life. Anton kept turning round in his chair and glaring at me. "What do you keep tutting at, loser?" Others joined him.

I hadn't realised I'd been tutting, but I had good reason – if only the rest of them knew what I had to put up with. Was this going to be my future, I thought? Was he going to follow me around all day every day messing up my life?

"Phew! School is hard," Grandad said when the bell went.

"It's a lot harder today than it's ever been before," I grumbled. "Now come on, we don't have much time."

As we arrived outside the jannie's office, Grandad introduced me to a side of himself I'd not yet seen: being useful.

"Why do I not go in first, check if the coast is clear?"

"Wow, good idea," I said. And for the first time I began to see the advantage of having a ghost on my side. Someone who could go places unnoticed, and sneak and snoop around without anyone seeing. Ask any great detective what's the one special power they'd like, and they'd all answer the same thing: invisibility.

Before he could go inside, the door pushed open. I slid behind a filing cabinet and hid.

I was fine there, except I soon found my ghostly grandad trying to squeeze in beside me. I felt a cold and damp sensation as his greenish skin pressed into mine.

I mouthed at him, "Go!" and shooed him away.

"Ha! Sorry, I forget I am a ghost sometimes. I do not need to hide."

A set of footsteps was walking in the other direction.

No, two sets. "It's OK," said Grandad. "It is safe to look, they are going away."

I peeked over the top of the cabinet to see two men, a fat man and a thin man. They were wearing blue boiler suits. One was carrying a large toolbox and the other a holdall with something large stuffed inside. "It is the two men from the CCTV," said Grandad, and he was right. They were both wearing the same beanie hats for a start. Now I was almost positive – Big Davie's death was no accident. It was linked to the body in the library. And what's more, if those two men had been in his office, it was for a reason. Well, there was one sure way to find out.

Grandad went in to case the joint, although I had to hold the door open for him first, which kind of defeated the purpose. I really hoped he would soon learn to just walk through things, like normal ghosts are supposed to do.

He called out from the other side, "The coast is clear."

The jannie's office was as messy as ever, but it wasn't hard to see that it had been thoroughly ransacked. All the drawers were half-open with documents and papers sticking out. I made a beeline for the CCTV.

At first glance, the bank of monitors looked just the same as they had the day before, but it didn't take me long to figure out what had changed. The hard drive was missing.

"Those guys must have taken it! The recording is gone," I said.

At that moment, the door behind us pushed open.

CHAPTER 11

The Sixth Sense

Grandad barked a warning: "JAYESH!"

I ducked under the CCTV control panel. My worst fear was that those two men had returned. If they were murderers, then they'd struck twice already, and what would stop them murdering again? I was sure I could talk my way out of pretty much anything, but I didn't want to take the risk.

It wasn't them. It was a man and a woman, chattering. I quickly recognised their voices.

"Oh, it's the guy your mother had in a headlock yesterday," said Grandad. It was the head teacher, Mr Kessock, along with the office manager, Mrs Cravat.

"There's nobody here! There's nobody here!" said Mr Kessock in his panicked nasal voice.

"Well, the stand-in janitor is probably off dealing with something else," replied Mrs Cravat.

"Oh, but what will I do?" he squeaked. "The new school handbook is being delivered. There are boxes and boxes of them, and the lorry's waiting outside. Police are swarming everywhere. If word gets out about our janitor 'problem'," he punched the air with his fist, "I'll NEVER win Head Teacher of the Year!"

Mrs Cravat sighed and made a calming motion with her hands. "Don't fret, Mr Kessock, we'll ask the delivery men to move the boxes into the strong room. It'll do for now."

They turned and left, and I crawled out from under the control panel.

"Boy, is that guy stressed!" said Grandad.

I gazed at Big Davie's desk. The printer he'd been working on was still sitting there, the screwdriver lying beside it.

"Poor Davie." Someone came after him because of what he knew; I was sure of it. What we'd found out together had made him a target.

All of a sudden I began to feel dizzy. I rushed outside, and didn't stop until I got into the fresh air. My legs wobbled on the school steps. I had to steady myself against the wall.

Grandad followed me out. "Ah, Jayesh," he said. He tried to put his arm around me, but it just passed straight through. The strange thing was that I felt it. It felt weird, like a small icy wave rushing through my body. "Yuck! Please don't do that, Grandad."

"Sorry," he said. The printer's lorry had backed up to the entrance, and men were wheeling off sealed boxes on dollies down a ramp. "We should go to the police."

"Are you joking?" I said. "They don't want to hear from me. As far as they're concerned there hasn't even been a crime. We're the only ones who saw that tape. And *you* don't count because you're not really here."

He shrugged. "Thanks a lot."

Something in the corner of my eye drew my attention. Call it instinct. Call it sixth sense. Call it my detective training. Call it what you will. I glimpsed a man across the street. An olive-skinned man wearing a black raincoat, fedora hat and dark glasses. And he was clearly watching the school.

I know when someone is trying to look inconspicuous. Some people make so much of an effort they look the exact opposite, and this guy was one of them.

He raised an object to his face. Was it a phone? Yes, and his fingers tapped on the screen. He was taking photos. But of what?

"See that?" I asked.

Grandad looked over, just as the man turned away and disappeared down a side street. "What? I did not see anything."

"Nothing," I said, for whoever he was he would have to wait; I had other things on my mind.

"What do we do now?" Grandad asked.

Two people had died in my school, one of them partly because of me. And my mum and granny had nearly been arrested. It was time to put my detective skills to good use. Plus, I had an invisible sidekick who might actually, if he really tried, be quite helpful.

The deliverymen wheeled out another stack of boxes. Their white lorry reminded me of the *Duke's Laundry* van we'd spotted on the CCTV. It wasn't the same vehicle of course. It was a different size, and had different branding:

Big A Printers
Pollockshields

But I knew where the trail led now. "We're going to *Duke's Laundry*."

CHAPTER 12

The Elvis Gorilla

After school, I took Grandad to the bus stop.

"This will be great!" he declared, rubbing his hands. "I have not been on a bus in years."

"You haven't done anything in years, Grandad. You've been dead."

On the way, I stopped in at the local library to google the address for *Duke's Laundry*. Mum says I can have my own phone when I get to high school. She doesn't want me becoming a 'slave to screens' just yet. Have I mentioned how annoying she is? I made Grandad wait outside.

The address was in Govanhill, which wasn't far.

When I got back outside, I found Grandad standing outside the Pound Shop. He seemed to be talking to someone and was bending over, laughing. Someone who was not there. He waved me towards him.

"Jayesh, look, it's my pal, old Jock."

"There's no one there, Grandad."

"Oh..." He paused for a second, as if he was listening to someone. "Right. He says all I need to do is blink, like this." Grandad blinked his eyes forcefully. All of a sudden I could see who he was talking to. Another ghost. A sad-looking old man wearing a cloth cap and a Mackintosh raincoat. "Can you see him?"

I exchanged nods with the ghost of the old man, which was quite awkward really, and something I'd never thought I would be doing in a million years.

"Ah, that is a great trick. So, I can blink and Jayesh can see other ghosts?"

The old man spoke in a faltering voice. "That's right, and you can blink them away too."

"Well that is just great," said Grandad. "And how are you keeping, Jock?"

"Well, I'm deid, as you can see."

"Ah, shame, that. And how is your Elsie?"

Old Jock raised his eyes heavenwards. "She's still alive. I'm supposed to be haunting her, but I think it's the other way about. She's in the pound shop. Pff, shoppin! I thought being deid I'd get a break from it, but no. Being deid is just the same as being alive, except hardly anybody can see you. The only good thing is you don't feel the cold."

"Why the Mac then?" said Grandad, nodding at old Jock's coat.

The old man shrugged. "It's what I kicked the bucket in. I've never cared for it, to be honest. I was on my way to the bookies and it was raining, so I just flung it on. Now I'm stuck wearing it forever." He sighed, and looked Grandad up and down. "Here, I like your jacket though."

"This?" said Grandad, lifting his tweed lapels. "It has

never quite fitted right." He stroked his transparent chin. "Here, how about we swap?"

"I don't see why not," said Jock. "Your tweed for my Mac?"

The two men swapped jackets. Grandad ran his finger down the seams and sized himself up in a shop window. "This is much better. I am starting to feel like a detective."

Old Jock leaned forward. "You better skidaddle before Elsie comes out the shop. She doesn't like me talking to other ghosts."

"Right you are, Jock," said Grandad. "See you around."

"Cheerie-bye," said Jock as we were moving away. "And don't forget to blink again, or your boy will be seeing ghosts everywhere."

"Right, OK," said Grandad, and he gave another firm blink.

With that, Jock was gone.

Surely my life couldn't get any stranger?

I hoped there wouldn't be any more delays, but I was wrong, because when we got to the bus stop, he saw someone else he recognised.

"Ha! Look! It is Winkie MacFadgeon!" he said. It was a decrepit old man of about seventy-five, with wispy white hair, who was resting on his walking stick and staring into a puddle. "Ah, Winkie! He was one of my best customers. Used to run a corner shop in Crossmyloof." Grandad leaned into the man's face, grinning. "How are you keeping Winkie? He doesn't look well."

Winkie didn't respond. Unfortunately for Grandad the man was still alive, though only just. Grandad scowled, then turned to me. "Ask Winkie how his piles are. He always suffered terrible piles."

I shook my head firmly. No chance was I going to open a conversation about problems with old men's bottoms among complete strangers at a bus stop.

"Oh, come on. It will be funny."

I mouthed at him: NO.

Grandad flew into a huff, and was in a bad mood after that. On the plus side, it meant he shut up for a few moments. The bus pulled up, and we got on.

I dropped my money into the slot and took my ticket. Grandad stepped up to the driver after me. "Do you have a discount for the deceased?" he said, laughing at his own joke. The driver of course didn't respond. He just shut the door and drove off.

Now Grandad was in a good mood again. He sat down next to me, rubbing his hands. "One of the benefits of being dead: free bus travel."

In spite of all this, Grandad was still acting like he was alive and everyone could see him. At one point, he got up to give his seat to a lady carrying heavy shopping. "There you go, Madam," he said, showing her the seat and smiling. Even though she was halfway through plonking herself down on the seat anyway.

Duke's Laundry was a double shopfront on the ground floor of a red sandstone tenement. It was grotty on the outside: boarded up windows, cracked walls and flaking paint. I dreaded to think what it looked like inside.

"You would think a laundry would be cleaner," said Grandad, and he was right. Why would anyone take their clothes to be cleaned in such a place?

I pushed open the door. There was a woman behind the counter. At least, she might have been a woman. She might also have been a gorilla that had been shaved, plastered in make-up and dressed in human clothes. But, I reckoned the chances of her being a woman were more likely. She also had pointy glasses and an Elvis haircut, which I didn't think would be the fashion choice of a sensible gorilla.

"Hello!" I gave her my widest, most winning smile.

The woman belched.

Baaarrrp

Or was it a growl? I couldn't be sure. Either way, she sounded like a bear with a sore throat. And an attitude problem. And, probably, a bad case of indigestion.

I stared around at the place, making sure to keep a well-meaning grin on my face. But there wasn't much to look at, just bare walls and a counter with a stack of paper on it. There wasn't even a price list on the wall that I could pretend to be interested in.

"What do you want?" Now she definitely was growling.

Grandad slipped behind the counter and stared at the woman in horror. "Jeezo, I would not like to meet her on a dark night."

I nodded in the direction of the open door behind her. Grandad winked, gave me the thumbs up and ducked through it. He was off to check out the back. This was good, I thought. Maybe the beginning of some kind of teamwork. I could definitely see how useful it would be having a ghost about, if only Grandad could *be* that useful.

I stepped towards the counter. Up close, I could see

that she had a wart the size of a fifty pence piece on her cheek. I had to think of something to say, but what? "Er, is this a laundry?"

"You tryin' to be funny?" She grunted.

"May I speak to Mr Duke, please?" I asked.

"Deid," she said.

"Are you the manager?"

"Whit's it to you?" She pulled a two-litre bottle of cola from behind the counter. It had a double straw poking out of the top. She wrapped her lips around the straw and started slurping. She took about half the bottle in one go. The sound of it running down her gullet was like water escaping down a plughole. She finished with another loud belch.

Bluuuuurrrp!

"You don't like customers very much, do you?" I asked.

Another door opened nearby, and out stepped two men. The same two men from the CCTV. One fat, one thin, both wearing their white overalls from the day before, and their beanie hats.

The short one was flat-nosed, round-headed, with one of those mouths that was constantly turned down in a frown. The tall one had ginger hair and freckles, and a pair of eyes that were too close together for their own good, or anyone else's. This made him look terrifying. He was glaring at me. They were both glaring at me. Glaring like a pair of misshapen hawks eyeing up their latest snack.

CHAPTER 13

The Dirty Laundry

The woman laughed. If you could call it a laugh. It sounded more like a walrus at feeding time. "No, we don't like customers here, do we boys?"

At the moment, I was just buying time. I didn't fancy my chances of getting any answers out of these people; they were too hostile. But there were ways of needling information, even out of the likes of them. And I was going to have to needle, because this place was definitely knee-deep in whatever shady business was going on at our school.

"Right, so, er, Mrs Duke?" I said.

"The name's Cleggan." She jabbed her thumb at the two men. "And these are Fred and Ginger."

This was good. I had names now.

The thin man, Ginger, sneered at me. "You call her Maw Cleggan."

"Maw?" I said, still trying on the charm. "What a lovely name. Is it Welsh?"

"Naw!" she honked. "Maw, as in, your maw! You daft twit."

"Right," I said, eyeing up the back door. How long was

Grandad going to be? "It's just that I'm doing a project at school, and I was hoping you could help?"

Doing a project at school was a gamble I used a lot. It was a good excuse to ask lots of questions. After all, who is going to suspect a schoolboy doing a project?

Maw Cleggan screwed up her face at me. "A project?"

"Yes."

"Whit, on dry cleaning?"

"Er, Yeah, that's it."

"Son, you've got to get out more."

I shrugged. She took a second slurp from the bottle, draining another third. "OK, shoot!"

I went through a bit of a panic. I hadn't thought this bit out. I was going to have to come up with some daft question, but what?

"So, uh, do you use water?"

She screwed up her face again. "For dry cleaning? Naw, that's how they call it dry, son." She gazed at Fred and Ginger and shook her head.

"Right, but if you don't use water, how do you get it clean?"

Maw Cleggan sighed. At least it might have been a sigh. It might also have been the sound an asthmatic orangutan makes after it climbs a tall tree. Her lip curled into a snarl. Her thick, greasy fingers clenched around a large stapler. I could see she'd had enough, and she was about to chuck the stapler at me. That's when I backed off and raised my hands.

"You know what, I can see you're busy, so I'll be off."

As luck would have it, that's also when Grandad reappeared from through the back. "Are you alright, boy?"

But he could see I wasn't. I was backing towards the door, waving and grinning through clenched teeth. Meanwhile, Maw Cleggan came out from behind the counter. She was wearing luminous yellow trainers.

"Fred, Ginger, show him what the pavement looks like," said Maw Cleggan. Fred and Ginger advanced on me. I flung open the door and was about to run for it. That's when Grandad stepped in.

"Watch this, boy!" He puffed out his cheeks and blew. It was amazing, like a wind had sprung up from nowhere. A stack of papers sitting on the counter fluttered into the air like confetti. It was just what I needed to distract Fred and Ginger, who were flailing their arms about trying to catch the paper.

"You idiots!" said Maw Cleggan, before taking another slurp of her cola.

"Come on, Jayesh," said Grandad. I held the door open for him and he floated out. I snatched one of the bits of paper out of the air as I left, and slipped it into my pocket.

We nipped across the road. I hoped the flow of traffic would put them off following us, even if the flying paper didn't.

"That was brilliant, what you did there," I said to Grandad. "You never told me you could do that."

"I was not sure myself until I did it."

69

"What else can you do? Because this could be useful."

He puffed his cheeks. "I am not sure, boy. I am kind of new at this ghost business."

It was a pity we couldn't find out all this stuff before, I thought. But we'd just have to learn as we went along. "So, what did you find back there?" I asked.

"Very little, and that includes cleaning. All the washers and dryers are empty, there's no laundry being done. Either business is very slow or..."

"Maybe Maw Cleggan wasn't joking," I said. "Maybe she really doesn't want customers."

Grandad stopped in his tracks, a shocked expression on his face. "What did you say there?"

"Maw Cleggan..."

"MAW CLEGGAN!" He whimpered like he'd just seen a, well, a ghost. Grandad rubbed his see-through hand down over his see-through face. "Maw Cleggan? Don't tell me we are mixed up with Maw Cleggan??"

"I take it you've heard of her then?" This was strange, as I hadn't.

"You forget, boy, that my cash-and-carry business was in this part of Glasgow. In my day, she ran half the gangs on the southside. Last I heard she was retired and living on the Costa del Sol."

That would explain why I hadn't heard of her. I knew the names of most of the gang bosses. I even knew some of them by their faces. I had made it my business to find these things out, in my efforts to find my Dad again. It also explained something else – why would anyone take their clothes to be cleaned in this place?

"There's no laundry being done in *Duke's Laundry*," I said.

"Huh?"

"It's a front. It's not really a laundry. It's fake."

"Ah, you mean it's some kind of money-laundering business," said Grandad. "You know what money-laundering is, don't you? It is when criminals take the cash from their crimes and put it through a fake business. It makes the cash seem legitimate and clean."

"Aha!" I said. "Which is exactly why she doesn't want customers. It's why the outside is so grotty – to put people off."

Grandad shook his head. "This is a murky business, Jayesh. You should not be involved in it. That woman is dangerous."

"I've got no intention of being involved any longer than I need to," I said. "I just need to find some evidence."

Before we rounded the corner a voice called out, "Oi!" A stern, firm voice. And a hand gripped my elbow and pulled me back.

CHAPTER 14

The Spooky Shakedown

It wasn't Fred or Ginger grabbing my elbow. It was a woman, not Maw Cleggan either. A set of grim, determined eyes sized me up.

"Aw, no!" said Grandad. "It's Morning Burial."

"Eh?" I grunted.

"I'm DI Dawn Graves," the woman said. "Remember me?"

It was the police detective from the school library brawl. She wouldn't let go of me.

"Dawn Graves? Morning Burial?" grinned Grandad. "Get it?"

I shot him a glare. He wasn't taking this seriously. And here I was, his own grandson, being collared by the cops.

"What are you doing here?" she asked, with a mixture of suspicion and disdain. I noticed the car door flung open behind her. A bland looking Ford, a standard unmarked police car. I cursed myself. I should have spotted that, except I was too busy escaping from Fred and Ginger.

I glanced back in the direction of the laundry then it all added up. DI Graves must be on a stakeout. The police were watching the laundry. They must be onto them already, but for what? The chances were it was nothing to do with the missing corpse or Davie's death, mainly because, as far as they were concerned, there *was* no missing corpse and Davie had suffered a tragic accident.

"Sorry, what do you mean?" I said, playing innocent.

Grandad cut in. "Do not tell her anything, boy. If you get dragged into a police investigation you might have to testify in court. And let me tell you, no one has ever lived to testify against Maw Cleggan. The story goes that most of her enemies are wrapped in concrete propping up the Kingston Bridge."

The Kingston Bridge was a huge motorway bridge crossing the Clyde, so that added up to a lot of dead witnesses. Grandad was right.

"I mean, what were you doing in that laundry?" she asked.

I shrugged. "It's a free country."

"Didn't see you go in with anything. And Govanhill is a long way to come just for a dry cleaner."

"Um," I scratched my head.

"Come on, think up some story!" said Grandad.

"I'm a scout. I'm trying to get sponsorship money," I said.

"What?" said Grandad. "That is pure rubbish!"

"Sponsorship for what?" she asked.

"A trip to Argentina. To see the gorillas."

"There are no gorillas in Argentina you fool," snapped Grandad.

Graves raised one eyebrow. "Argentinian gorillas?"

"They're in a zoo," I said, calmly.

"So, where is your scout's uniform?" replied Graves.

"It's at the dry cleaners."

Another figure stepped out of an alley behind me. It was Constable McBurnie. His truncheon was drawn and there was a look of excitement on his face. "Is he a criminal, Boss? Can I clobber him with this?" He swung the baton like a propeller.

DI Graves sighed and rolled her eyes. "No, Constable. Get back in the alley. You're giving yourself away."

"Uch!" McBurnie's shoulders slumped, and he traipsed back into cover in a huff. "It's no' fair!"

Graves tightened her grip on my elbow. "Listen, son, I don't like you. Know why?"

"You're jealous of my winning personality?"

Grandad sucked his teeth. "Careful!"

"No, I don't like the same faces showing up in different places, it's suspicious."

"Huh! She is a charmer," said Grandad.

She let go of my elbow. It felt like being released from a vice. "I'll be watching out for you." She pointed her first and middle fingers to her eyes and then jabbed them in my direction. "Watchin'!"

With that, she got back into her car and slammed the door.

"Phew!" said Grandad as we hurried down the street. "So, the police must have cottoned on to Maw Cleggan's operation, eh?"

74

"Yup." I turned up a flight of steps and ducked down, peeking back over the wall towards the police car and the laundry.

"What are you doing?" said Grandad. "We should be getting back. I am beat."

I stared up at him. "How can you be beat? You're not even alive."

"Ghosts can get tired. That wind blowy thing really took it out of me."

"Well, we're not going yet," I said. "We've got to try and find that white van. It's our best link to the dead body. If we find that, we might be able to tip off the police. There might be evidence. The body might even still be in it. Or, at least, they can do forensics. If we can do that, then we might be able to step out of this whole thing."

"That sounds good to me," replied Grandad, "because you do not want to be involved with Maw Cleggan."

I gazed along the line of vehicles parked on each side of the high street. The white van was definitely not there. Parking would be difficult as it was a busy street... or maybe they deliberately parked the van further away.

"Grandad, do you fancy taking a walk round the block there, see if the van is parked in one of the side streets?"

"Sure. What about you?"

I had another idea to follow up – one that very quickly proved to be right.

CHAPTER 15

The Van Deduction

There was a big supermarket car park along the road. I figured a lot of people in the area would use it for parking. And that's exactly where I found the van, nose-first against a low wall.

Grandad had completed his circuit of the block and found nothing, then met me there.

"How did you know?" he asked.

I explained, and he grinned and nodded. "That is my clever boy."

I strolled around the vehicle, scrutinizing it closely, soaking up every detail I could find. By the time I'd come back round I had all the answers I needed.

"I'd say they've done away with the body already. In fact, I know exactly where it is."

"Pff! Rubbish!" said Grandad. His faith in my abilities was astounding.

"They buried it in a shallow grave up the country park."

"How could you possibly know that?"

"It's the best spot within twenty miles. If I had to get rid of a body that's where I'd hide it. In fact, there's a thick bit of woodland called Hagg's Pocket. That would be perfect."

"So? That is all guesswork, Jayesh," he said, folding his arms.

"C'mere," I knelt down to point out the reddish dust marks on the wheel arches. "See that? There's a road made of red gravel there. It's quite unusual. That's where this dust has come from."

Grandad gazed at me in disbelief. "Away you go!"

"Sherlock Holmes was an expert on tobacco ash, you know. He could identify one hundred and forty different types of ash."

"So? You are an expert on road dust now?"

"What do you think I've been doing these last nine months?" I said. "Sitting on my hands? I had to ask myself, what would the great detectives be doing? Would they be doing the same, or would they be swotting up on every piece of information possible?" I added, "It's a quiet spot. They did it about ten to six last night."

"Oh, come on, boy," he said. "I mean, I can believe the red dust thing, but how could you possibly know that?"

"Oh," I said, "I forgot to show you the most important piece of evidence." I led Grandad round the front and pointed out a car-parking ticket stuck to the inside of the windscreen. "You have to pay to park in the country park now."

"What?" he cried. "What a rip-off!"

"They might have been burying a dead body, but they're very law abiding, these two. I'm guessing they didn't want any unwanted attention from the parking attendants, just in case. The ticket says it ran out this morning at nine forty-four. You only have to pay up until six, and after that, if you've got any time left over, it rolls onto the next day. So, that means they arrived there at five forty-four yesterday afternoon. That's not long after they picked up the body. They must have taken it straight there."

Grandad puffed out his cheeks. "Well, I must say, Jayesh, I am impressed. I do not know where you got these brains from; not from your father, that is for sure."

"They're sloppy, these two," I added. "I would've washed the van by now, and cleaned out the inside. And if they haven't washed the outside then I'm guessing the inside hasn't been done either."

I unzipped the inside pocket of my parka and whipped out a piece of special equipment that I always carried with me: a plastic, thirty-centimetre ruler. I flexed it. Its bendiness was its greatest quality. It was perfect for what I wanted to do next.

I rammed it down inside the gap in the driver's window.

"What are you doing, Jayesh?" Grandad gasped, looking this way and that.

"I'm a detective. Detectives snoop. Keep an eye out, will you?"

A few seconds of jiggling was all it took for the button to pop up. I flicked the end of my sleeve over my fingers to avoid leaving fingerprints, then opened the door and crawled inside.

The van's interior was a mess: empty juice cans, crisp packets, newspapers and parking tickets. I poked around a bit, then slipped over the seats into the back.

There was a treasure trove of forensic evidence in here, and I didn't want to disturb it too much. I didn't want to leave *my* forensic evidence all over it either, so I unzipped one of the pockets on my arm and pulled out another piece of equipment that I took with me everywhere: a pair of surgical gloves. I pulled them on, and started rooting around in the mess.

Grandad squeezed his head through the back door.

"Urgh!" he said.

"You gave me a fright!" I said.

"Sorry! I really HATE passing through solid things!" he said. "What are you looking for?"

Aside from the two dirty spades, there was a whopper of a piece of evidence: a plastic bag holding keys and a wallet.

I flipped the wallet open, and pulled out bank cards, loyalty cards, a business card and even a driver's licence. The picture on the card was of a man with ginger hair and a beard. His name was James Morrison. The business card said he worked at a place called:

James Morrison
Sales Executive

MARLIN SHIPPING AGENTS

Tel
0141 6783452

Email
James@marlinshipping.co.uk

Website
www.marlinshipping.co.uk

"That's our man."

I'd hit the jackpot, and my face must have shown it. Grandad chortled. "You are smug! But well done, boy."

They say that pride comes before a fall, although in my case it was more of a bust, as at that moment, Grandad suddenly groaned and turned white. That's if it's possible for a ghost to turn white. Perhaps a paler shade of green than usual.

The doors of the van flung open. Standing there, on top of Grandad, glowering at me with menace, were the two men I hoped least in the world to see at that moment – Fred and Ginger.

CHAPTER 16

The Sneeze Escape

The tall man's mouth curled up into a sneer.

"Well, lookee here," he said. "We've got a sneak on us."

"Aye," said Fred. "A sneaky sneak thief. Looks like we've got him exactly where we want him n'all."

The two men laughed. "No escape," said Ginger.

Unfortunately, they were right. Here I was in the back of their van. All they had to do was slam the doors shut and drive off. I'd be pushing up the daisies in the country park within half an hour. Unless...

I gazed pleadingly at Grandad. "Do something!"

"I am on it!" He turned and ran. At first, I thought he might be abandoning me, but then I saw he was running in the direction of a woman. She was carrying a gigantic bunch of flowers and heavy shopping, and was being dragged along by two huge white dogs on a lead.

Grandad flailed his arms and moaned: "Ooooh! Waaaaaahh!"

I've never seen anything like it. The dogs went berserk. They said dogs have a sixth sense, but now I knew it was true. They barked frantically. One dog bolted in one direction. The other took off the opposite way. It was too much for the woman, whose arms were stretched apart as the dogs pulled. She screamed:

"AAAAARGH!"

Her bunch of flowers catapulted into the air, exploding in colour. Purple and white petals scattered everywhere, falling like a blizzard across the tarmac.

Grandad sneezed. That was weird, I briefly thought. How could a ghost possibly have allergies?

Fred and Ginger turned away, startled. It was a small distraction, no more than a glimpse of a chance. But it was all I needed.

I slipped over the seats, jumped out the front door and vaulted the low wall of the car park. Before the two men knew what was happening I was sprinting up the street.

I glanced over my shoulder. The chubby one was struggling to get over the wall, so him I didn't have to worry about. But the skinny one was right behind me, and gaining fast.

The high street was busy. There were lots of obstacles. Each one was an opportunity. I only hoped I could avoid them all myself. I skipped past a team of burly deliverymen wheeling a washing machine out of the electrical shop. I dodged round a gaggle of women wearing burkhas. I weaved in-between the people queuing for the bus.

Next was a short, tubby old lady carrying heavy shopping – one of those tiny grannies that somehow manages to take up an entire pavement. I slid through the gap between one of her shopping bags and the wall.

I cast a hopeful glance behind me, only to find that none of these obstacles had held Ginger back one bit. He just barged through everyone, leaving a lot of angry people shaking their fists in his wake.

I pulled off my surgical gloves and threw them at him. He swotted them aside. I passed a hardware store with lots of bins and storage boxes sitting outside. I kicked them into his path, but he just leapt over them.

The next shop was a greengrocers, with lots of fruit and vegetables in display boxes. I kicked over a tray of watermelons, which splattered the ground in front of his feet. He shimmied through them. I picked up some yellow melons and tossed them at his head. They missed,

although they did hit the old lady with the shopping, who yelped and fell backwards into a steel dustbin. Her legs splayed up into the air.

The greengrocer herself came running out, a woman wearing a hijab. She was screaming and carrying a baseball bat. "My fruit! My fruit!" She swung at Ginger, a pretty lethal swing as well. If it had been a baseball she was hitting she'd be on a home run. But he ducked under the bat and kept running. Would nothing stop this man?

I thought all was lost, but then Grandad reappeared at my side.

"Here is a florist!" he said, as we reached the next shop. The front was festooned with flowers. "Let us try another experiment!" He ducked his spectral head right into the middle of them, then pulled it out again.

He clutched his face. It looked ready to explode, and so it did, just as he turned towards my pursuer.

AHHHHH-CHOOOOO!

Grandad's colossal sneeze kicked up a load of litter and dust and shot it into Ginger's face. He threw up his arms to protect himself. But even a sneeze from a ghost wasn't enough! He still kept coming.

I was seriously worried now. He was just metres away, and on the verge of grabbing me. Then a man staggered out of the pub. A large man with a bulgy crimson nose. I span him round and pushed him into Ginger. The two of them collapsed on the pavement, the large man spread out on top of him.

As I darted across the road, I glanced back again, to see the man from the pub hauling Ginger to his feet.

"Are you wantin' a fight, mate?" The man swung, Ginger ducked. Then the man grabbed him round the middle and they started wrestling on the pavement.

Grandad was standing nearby, laughing. He gave me the thumbs up and waved me on. I was free!

I turned up a path into a graveyard. Not an ideal place to go if you are trying to avert death, but it was a good place to hide. There was lots of cover. And they couldn't follow me in the van. Besides, I knew this graveyard. It had lots of exits at different ends, and one of them led onto the main road where I could catch the bus home.

I found a spot in the bushes near the exit next to my bus stop, where I took a rest. As luck would have it, no sooner had I settled into my hiding spot than a bus appeared. I made it on to the bus and collapsed into the back seat, gazing fearfully out the rear window. It didn't matter how far away I got from *Duke's Laundry*, from Fred and Ginger and their white van of death, I was still scared.

They knew me now. They knew my face. I was no longer inconspicuous. The bad guys were on to me.

CHAPTER 17

The Small-time Detective

Back home, there was no sign of Grandad. Not that I was worried. He knew the way home. Besides, he was dead already, so what was the worst that could happen?

Mum was in the kitchen cooking tea.

"Hullo, dearie!" she yelled, and wrapped her arms around me. "Where have you been? Your dinner's nearly ready."

Mum turned to the stove and whipped the lid off the pot. "Ta-daaa! Himalayan aubergine curry."

Yeti vomit.

I tried to look pleased. "Yum." To be honest, I could have murdered a chicken burger.

Mum picked up a small mallet and whacked a gong. Yes, an actual gong. One of Mum's favourite pieces of décor was a small gong, which she'd brought back from a yoga retreat in Goa. She said she liked the sound it made, and besides, Granny was hard of hearing so it helped get her attention.

Even so, Granny still hadn't heard it, as she was busy re-tiling the bathroom. "Granny! Dinner's ready!"

The bathroom floor was littered with tiles and tools, and covered in dust. Granny poked her head out of the shower cubicle. She was wearing flip-flops, a bathing costume, swimming goggles and a shower cap.

"WHIT?!" She was cradling a tile in one hand and a trowel in the other.

"Why?" I asked, nodding down at her outfit.

"Ah'm gonnie have a shower afterwards," she croaked.

It was only after dinner that Grandad got back.

"Jayesh!" I heard a muffled call from the hall.

I ran out to find one of his legs poking through the front door. Then an arm, then the other arm and a head. "Urgh!" He took a deep breath and hauled himself inside, then shivered. "Yuck! I HATE doing that!"

"What happened to you?" I whispered.

"I decided to stick around, so I could see where those two went."

"Good," I said. "And?"

"Oh-ho, you put the wind

up them, that is for sure. They wondered if you knew something about the body, but they were not sure. One of them kept saying, 'Oh, he's just a boy, he's just a boy, what does he know?' They were talking about setting the van on fire. And then one of them said they should dump it in the Clyde. Then they got hungry, so they went for a McDonalds instead."

It was annoying that they had caught me when they did, because it put the evidence at risk. If they did set fire to the van, or dump it in the water, then lots of vital clues might be lost. I reckoned they would at least wash it now, they might even clean the inside out. They'd certainly ditch the shovels and the dead man's wallet and keys. But even if they did, a good forensics team might still be able to find evidence.

Grandad flopped down on the sofa. "And it took me ages to get home. Have you ever tried flagging down a bus when you're invisible?

I rummaged in my pocket, not really listening. I remembered dropping the driving licence and wallet as I escaped the van, but there was one thing I had the presence of mind to keep – the dead man's business card.

"Aha!" said Grandad as I held the card up in my fingers and twiddled it around. "So, are we going to do it?"

"Do what?" I asked.

"Tip off the police?"

"Yes." We had more than enough information to pass to

the cops now. Then, maybe, I could step out of this thing. It was getting too dangerous for a small-time detective like me.

And we had to be fast. I could tell them where I thought the body was buried, but for all I knew Fred and Ginger could be on their way to the country park right now to move it somewhere else. If I was in their shoes, and I knew someone might be on to me, that's exactly what I would do, just in case.

I checked Mum's room. She was sitting on her bed in the lotus position. Sitar music was playing, incense and candles burning, and the lights were down low. Her eyes were closed, her hands were raised, her forefingers and thumbs pinched together, and she was chanting "OMMMMM!" over and over again.

How she managed to meditate with Granny around was a mystery, as Granny had just fired up an angle grinder. She was attacking tiles with a high-pitched screech, and, just to be clear, the screeching was *her*.

"AIEEEEEE!!!"

A massive white cloud of dust engulfed her, billowing into the hall.

"A handy woman, your granny," said Grandad. "She always was."

"Let's go," I said, and we nipped out the front door.

Half a mile up the road there was a phonebox. There was one closer, but I decided to use one further away, just in case they tried to trace me.

I picked up the handset. "Well, here goes."

Grandad nodded. "Go on boy, phone it in."

A voice came over the line: "Hello, Directory Enquiries."

"Pollockshields Police Station, please."

CHAPTER 18

The Wandering Accent

I waited, dry-mouthed, as the phone rang. I wanted to give them enough info to find the body, but not so much that they could connect it in any way to me.

"Hello, police?" came a tough, no-nonsense sort of a voice, the voice of a front-line copper.

Only now did it occur to me that I should disguise my accent somehow. I only had a split-second to think about it. I'm not sure why, but the accent I went with was upper-class English.

"Ah, good h-eeevening, my maahn!" I said. "I e-have some information."

Grandad stared at me in open-mouthed disbelief. I went on, "There is a bod-eh buried in the country p-hark. Try the wh-oodl-end at H-eggs P-hocket."

"What's this?" replied the voice. "A body? Who is this?"

"N-hever y-hoo moynd." I bit my tongue. That last word made me sound like a cider farmer from Somerset. "*Moynd*," I repeated. It still came out the same way. I decided to go with it. "Deh registrashiin numbur..." I cringed. Now I just sounded Irish. It seemed I couldn't do a Somerset accent either. I cursed myself, realising I should have practised this first. "The registration is X... L...9, 4... B... W." For some reason the 'W' came out in a kind of Texan drawl: "double-yea-oouu."

"Are you American?" said the voice.

Again, I decided just to go with it. It was still better than them thinking I was from Pollockshields.

"Uh, y-ay-as, pardner. Now, why don't y'all jus' head on down there an' round 'em up."

I hung up and breathed a long sigh of relief. "Phew!"

Grandad's head was sunk into his hands. "That was pathetic, boy!" he said. "You did a world tour there. Do they not teach drama in that school?"

I shook my head. I was too tired to argue. "C'mon, let's go home." I'd told the police where the body was, and I'd given them the registration of Fred and Ginger's van. Surely they could work out the rest themselves.

I was tired. It was all catching up on me now. It had been a LONG day.

Maybe now, I thought, I could sit back and let the police do their job.

CHAPTER 19

The Haunted Mask

The following morning, I bolted down breakfast and grabbed my schoolbag. "Bye Mum! Bye Granny!"

Mum didn't hear. She was up to her elbows in flour, making dough for some kind of weird cake from her *Eco Mum Cookbook*. It had beetroot in it. I have no idea why. Maybe she thought I needed more fibre in my diet.

Granny strutted past wielding a giant roll of loft insulation. We don't even have a loft, so I'm not sure what she was planning to do with it. "Cheerie-bye!" she croaked.

Grandad was already outside on the landing, talking to someone who wasn't there. He blinked his eyes at me, and a tubby old lady carrying a net shopping bag appeared. Cheery and smiley though she was, she was very blotchy and wonky-looking. Grandad didn't seem to notice, or it didn't appear to bother him. "Look, it's Isa McClutcheon, as I live and breathe." He caught himself on. "Well, you know."

"Och, I'm like that myself, Sanjeev," laughed the old lady. "I keep forgetting that I'm deid."

Just look in the mirror, I thought. That'll remind you.

Grandad winked. "You know, me and Isa, we used to be sweethearts, a long time ago."

Isa gave a flirty, high-pitched laugh, and her head fell back – no, literally, it was hanging off. She had to reach behind her and flip it back over. "Och, ye naughty man, look what you've done."

"Well, we'd better be off, Isa," said Grandad, following me down the stairs. "See you around."

I was in a hurry to get to school and see if my tip-off last night had come to anything. I hadn't mentioned the school in my call, but surely if they did act on it, and they did find the body, then someone at the police station would put two and two together and connect it to the body that went missing from the school library.

"Hold on! I am coming with you!" said Grandad, rushing to keep up as I bounded down the stairs.

When I got to school, I saw something that gave me a flicker of confidence in Pollockshields police. By that I mean, they were actually there. They'd worked it out. There were at least three squad cars and a big van marked 'Forensic Investigations'. A crowd of kids were hanging round, watching and wondering what was going on.

"Aha! So, it worked," said Grandad.

"Looks like it."

I expected that Mum would get pulled in at some point, either to the school or to the police station. She was the one who reported the body, so she was their chief witness,

and they would want to interview her. What I wasn't
expecting was for them to come for me.

It was Mr Kessock who appeared at the door of the class
and spoke my name.

"Jayesh Patel, my office - now!"

He was practically hyperventilating and I knew by the
super-sour-lime-sucking look on his face that it was to do
with the cops. My heart sank. I must have made a mistake
somewhere, I thought, but where?

"I knew it! It's Patel they're after," whispered Anton, as
I made my way down through the row of desks. "Probably
for his bad dress sense."

Nobody laughed at his joke, which gave me a small
sense of satisfaction. Except for Pyotr, and that was only
because he was watching a video on his phone.

Mwah-hah-hah-heeeeee!

"Maybe your mother told them something," said
Grandad, as I walked behind Mr Kessock towards the
office, but what? She didn't know anything.

Or maybe it's because DI Graves caught me outside
Duke's Laundry. If they had tracked the registration
number to that place, then I guess it would put me in an
awkward position. As it turned out I wasn't even half right.

"I'm up for Head Teacher of the Year, you know," said Mr Kessock through gritted teeth just before he pushed open the office door.

"Yes, we know," me and Grandad replied at the same time.

"He doesn't shut up about that, does he?" said Grandad.

Kessock pointed his finger right into my face. "You better not ruin things for me, that's all."

Mrs Cravat glared at me as I came into the office. DI Graves was sitting behind the desk. Boy, her face was grim. The kind of grim you only get in Glasgow; that comes from bad weather and too many fish suppers.

Constable McBurnie was there too, propped up against the wall, his thumbs hooked into his utility belt, and his hat pushed down over his forehead, looking like a gunslinger hanging about outside a saloon in the Wild West.

A large African tribal mask hung on the wall, with two empty hooks underneath. It was a fearsome thing, a gift from our twin school in Africa. I felt its open-mouthed stare drilling into me. Grandad felt it too; in fact it really freaked him out. He shivered when he saw it.

"Wo-ho! That mask is seriously haunted."

Constable McBurnie saw me glance at the mask. He eyed it up too, and poked it with his finger.

"Don't touch that!" snapped Mrs Cravat. "That's a priceless piece of art, from the Mumbari people."

McBurnie grinned like a maniac and poked it again. Mrs Cravat stared back at him, her lips pursed and her eye twitching.

"I mean it," said Grandad. "That thing is ogling me, and it is very annoyed about something. Spirit energy is flowing out of it. This woman who guards it does not even know."

Graves waved a hand at McBurnie, and he stepped away from the mask. Then she nodded Mrs Cravat towards the door. "Thank you, Madam, that will be all for now."

Mrs Cravat stiffened and walked out. Graves stretched out her leg and kicked a chair out for me. "Sit."

"Uh-oh, she means business," said Grandad, as I perched on the chair.

And she did.

CHAPTER 20

The Chicken's Neck

DI Graves gazed at me from under her heavy eyelids, much as a vulture might eye up a smaller bird who happened to be pecking around nearby.

"We found a body," she said eventually.

If she was expecting a reaction from me then she was wrong. I wasn't exactly calm inside, more terrified really, but I was determined my face wouldn't betray me.

"A body?" I asked, faking a shocked look.

"In the country park. Same description as the one your mum reported in the library." She nodded through the wall. The library was just next door.

"Oh dear," I said. "Who was it?" She thought she was interviewing me, but that wasn't altogether true. I was probing her to find out how much information she had.

"We don't know yet. We're working on it."

"Hmm... but how would it have got from the library to the country park?" I wanted to know if they had tracked down the van? She stared at me intensely for a few seconds, as if she was trying to force me to blink.

Meanwhile, Grandad let out a wail so loud I jumped.

"Aaaaahhh!!"

Graves' eyebrows screwed up. And McBurnie's entire face. I glanced over at Grandad, to see him pointing at the mask in terror. "Jayesh! Jayesh! There are ghosts coming out of that mask."

Whoever these ghosts were, he forgot that I couldn't see them. Which was just as well, as I was too busy being interrogated.

Graves eyed me for a moment, then went on. "We got a tip-off last night. The registration number of a white van. Trouble is, that registration was for a Nissan Micra belonging to a vicar in Basingstoke, which was reported stolen last month. So, not much use."

I could have kicked myself. I should have known Maw Cleggan would be using a stolen licence plate. So, the cops hadn't been able to trace the body to *Duke's Laundry*.

Grandad's wailing was getting louder.

"Aaaaaarrghhh!"

I glanced round to see him edging back towards the door, holding his palms up defensively and looking about him, as if he was being pushed.

"Now, look here, gentlemen, I can see that you are angry, but it has nothing to do with me. I am dead too…"

"Tell me something," said Graves. She unscrewed the tip off a **Big A Printers** pen like she was slowly wringing a chicken's neck. "What were you doing hanging about the janitor's office at lunchtime yesterday?"

Again, I could have kicked myself. Someone had spotted me. Not for the first time, I would just have to bluff my way out.

"I was looking for the sick bucket," I replied.

She leaned forward. "Someone tampered with the CCTV. The hard drive is missing. We think whoever did it might be involved in the murders."

Suddenly, I did not like the way this interview was headed. If they thought I tampered with the CCTV then there was a good chance they also saw me as a suspect.

"Murder*s*?" I asked.

"Yes, I shouldn't have to tell you that the death of your school janitor is now being treated as suspicious as well."

No, she didn't have to tell me. I could have told *her*. There was something more than suspicious about Big Davie's death. What was really worrying me at the moment was that I was being linked with it. With both murders in fact. And Mum too.

Grandad now had his back against the wall, and was pushing up on his tiptoes, as if looking over a crowd. He was fanning them with his hands. "Gentlemen, calm down, please!" He shot me a pleading look. "Jayesh, are you seeing this? Oh, sorry, I forgot, hold on."

Grandad clenched his eyes and gritted his teeth. Was he doing what I thought he was about to do?

"NO!" I shouted.

Graves stared at me like I was dressed in a chicken costume, wearing a sign that said:

Please wring
my neck
for me now

"No?" said Graves.

Suddenly, I liked this interview even less – in the blink of an eye the room was full. A dozen men wearing tribal robes and carrying spears were all shouting angrily, yelling themselves hoarse in an African language, and pointing in our faces, including Graves and McBurnie's – not that they noticed.

"They call themselves the Mumbari," said Grandad. "These guys are the ancestors of the tribe."

Whoever he was, the guy who was currently looming in my face must have suffered one humdinger of a death, as his right eyeball was dangling out of its socket.

The Key Suspect

"See?" said Grandad. "Now you know why I hate other ghosts?"

"Eh, hullo?" DI Graves was gazing at me like I had ripped off the chicken costume to reveal a sparkly green leotard with purple leggings underneath, and another sign that read:

Are you sure you wouldn't like to wring my neck for me now?

I buried my head in my hands. "Will you PLEASE stop!" I was talking to Grandad, but I could just as easily have been talking to any of them.

"What?" Graves asked threateningly.

McBurnie whipped out his truncheon. "Can I hit him for that?"

She dismissed him with a wave of her hand. "Oh, come on," he moaned. "He's asking for it."

"Sorry!" Grandad called out from within the tangle of ghostly bodies. "Just wanted you to see what I have to put up with."

When I looked up, the shouting men were all gone. It was just the living again, and Grandad. I would've breathed a sigh of relief, except I wasn't that relieved. I'm not sure the living, in this case, were that much friendlier than the dead.

Graves tapped the pen against the lip of the **Big A** mug sitting on the desk in front of her. "The tip-off was an anonymous one. It came from a public phonebox not far from here. We checked it out, of course. We got one eyewitness."

An eyewitness, I thought, biting my lip. How unlucky was that? This was getting worse by the moment.

Graves picked up her notebook and flicked through it. "A darkly-clothed figure, about four foot ten..." She looked me up and down purposefully. "The witness thought the figure seemed to be having an argument with himself."

Grandad chortled from over in the corner. "Oh, you have no idea, lady!"

"So," said Graves, screwing the lid back on the pen, then plucking it off with a POP – like it was the chicken's head, or *my* head. "Do you have anything to tell me?"

She clasped her hands and gazed at me expectantly. This was the moment she'd been building up to. She laid all the evidence out in front of me and then challenged me to come clean.

"NO!" Grandad appeared at my shoulder, struggling as if fighting the ghostly men off. "Jayesh! Do not tell them about Maw Cleggan. Unless they get hold of that van then you have got nothing on her. She will be free by five o'clock and by half past you will be floating to the bottom of the Clyde wearing concrete ankle boots."

But, if I didn't tell her everything, then what evidence she had linked the murders to me and my mum. I was seen in the jannie's office when the CCTV was swiped, and someone who looked like me was spotted phoning in the anonymous tip-off.

And yet, the longer I sat there, twiddling my thumbs under the detective's gaze, the more it became clear that Grandad was right. I stood up.

"Sorry, I can't help you."

McBurnie lurched forward. "Can I batter him, Boss? Ah, go on, just a wee tap on the nut?"

"No," said Graves. She stood up briskly and pressed a business card into my hand. "For when you change your mind."

Graves nodded at the door, signalling the interview was over, but then she called me back. "Oh, and you should know, your mother is at the police station. She's helping us with our enquiries."

"Is she under arrest?" I asked.

"She's the only one who saw the body. So, until we find more evidence, she's a key witness. And… a key suspect." She shrugged, and tilted her head, knowingly. Another challenge. But I didn't rise to it.

"What!" cried Grandad. "You have arrested my daughter-in-law?"

"Think about it. She's the one who reported the body," I said. "Why would she commit a murder and then report it herself?"

"You'd be surprised what people do," said Graves, "to dodge suspicion." She slammed the door in my face.

I raced up the corridor, leaving Grandad banging his fists at the office door, or at least trying to; his hands were just going through it, and making no noise whatsoever. "How dare you accuse poor Katie! I'll haunt you if you do not watch out."

Was DI Graves holding Mum deliberately to make me talk? Or was she really about to try and pin Morrison's murder, and Big Davie's too, on us? Well, that wouldn't happen, because I had other plans.

Grandad floated up behind me as I passed through the main school gate. "Phew! Maybe I am getting used to this floating business, uh?" he said. "Where are we going?"

I looked around to make sure we weren't being followed. The only thing that stood out was the man in the fedora hat and overcoat, the one I'd seen the other day taking photos. He was perched on the wall across from the entrance writing in a notebook, but he wasn't interested in me. He was watching the school. What was he up to? Whatever it was, I didn't have time to hang around and find out. I had enough on my plate.

"The police don't know the identity of the body. It won't be long before they do. That gives us a chance." I flagged down an approaching bus.

"A chance for what?" said Grandad.

"To find out who James Morrison was, and why he was killed."

CHAPTER 22

The Bamboozled Turnstile

On the bus, I turned James Morrison's business card over in my fingers. I still had no idea what linked him to our school. Or what linked him to Maw Cleggan. Or, for that matter, how Maw Cleggan was linked at all. Come to think of it, I didn't know very much. But I still knew more than the police.

Murder, money-laundering, whatever it was, it was a dark business.

Morrison was a shipping agent, or, at least, he used to be, when he was alive. As far as I knew that was something to do with importing and exporting goods by sea, handling shipments of cargo, that kind of thing. Maybe he was crooked? Maybe that's how he was linked with organised crime. Maybe he was smuggling something into the country: drugs, gold, even people.

Or, maybe he wasn't crooked at all. Maybe he was straight, and he'd found something out. Either way, what made him come to the school and why had he been killed there?

So many questions, and if I was going to put Mum

and me in the clear for the two murders then I was going to have to get some answers – and fast!

MARLIN SHIPPING was on the fourth floor of a drab concrete office building. From the looks of it, I wouldn't get past the reception desk. They had a security guard and turnstiles, which were operated by the employees' ID cards. But it wouldn't be a problem for Grandad.

"Go up there and have a snoop. See if you can find Morrison's desk," I said to him.

"Rely on me, boy," he said. He raised his hands to his eyes, as if to fix an imaginary pair of glasses, then tutted. "Wish I had my shades." Then he floated through the glass entrance doors.

As the minutes ticked by, I decided to scout the building. A set of steps led down to an underground car park. There was another entrance around the back, with a security card reader and a turnstile, but no security guard. I hung around there, watching the folk who worked there coming and going, scanning their cards as they went. I wondered how hard it would be to nick one.

I went into the SPAR, bought a can of cola, some chocolate and a bunch of flowers, then I returned to the front of the office building where Grandad had left me, and waited.

It was another ten minutes before he re-appeared, floating out of the lift, then through the glass doors.

"Uuuuugh!"

"I found his desk," he said. "It is one of these fancy open-plan offices, but there is no one sitting nearby. There was a little bronze plaque with his name on it."

"And?"

"And what?" he replied. "It's a desk. There is nothing on it. The drawers do not look like they are locked. You could probably open them, but not me."

Not being able to touch anything was a serious drawback to being a ghost. I would have to get in there myself. But it was alright, I'd already thought of a plan.

"Come on, Grandad." I led him round to the rear entrance.

"What's this?" he asked.

"You'll see." We waited there until I saw someone leaving with a Marlin ID card in her hand, a rotund woman wearing a black coat.

Just as she was about to pass I shoved the flowers under Grandad's ghostly nose. "Smell these."

"What!" he cried, before launching into a colossal sneeze.

AHHHHH-CHHOOO!

I braced myself, ready to pounce.

A huge gust of wind caught the woman off balance. She staggered and fell over, landing on her bottom. The contents of her handbag scattered across the pavement.

I rushed over to help her to her feet. "Are you OK, Missus?"

She looked up gratefully, which she wouldn't have done if she'd known I was the one to blame. "Oh, dear, what was that, son?" She got to her feet and brushed herself down. "The wind just blew up from nowhere."

"Oh well, that's Glasgow weather for you," I said, picking her stuff off the pavement and cramming it back into her handbag. "Here, have these, you deserve them." I thrust the flowers at her.

"Oh, thank you, son," She looked dazed as she turned to totter down the road.

Grandad was staring at me with a strange, quizzical look.

I dangled the lanyard in front of him, with her ID card on the end. "Ta-da!" I put it round my neck.

"So now, if anyone asks..." he said, leaning forward to read the card. "You are Susan Maguire, Input Analyst."

"That's me! Input analysis is my bag." I grinned. So did he.

"Clever boy."

"After you," I said. "You can show me the way."

The ID badge got me through the security door and the turnstile, and up to the fourth floor in the lift. On the way, I tore off my school sweatshirt and tie. Hopefully I wouldn't look too out of place, apart from the fact I was only eleven.

"Oh, I forgot to tell you," said Grandad, as we stepped out of the lift into a wide foyer. "There's a second turnstile, and you need a pin number for it."

"But I don't have a pin," I said. "Why didn't you tell me this before we came up here?"

I was annoyed, because here I was standing on the landing outside the **MARLIN SHIPPING** office, in front of a turnstile which I couldn't get through. Sooner or later someone was going to notice me here, and send me away. I needed to keep moving.

"Oho! Let me try something." He pinched his nose with his fingers and closed his eyes, as if he was about to jump into a swimming pool feet first. And then, he did actually jump. His ghostly form swirled about, then disappeared like water down a plughole, shooting into the turnstile's keypad.

The turnstile bleeped. A green light came on, and I pushed my way through.

Grandad shot out of the other side and wobbled about on the floor. "Haaayyy! I am not doing that again." He had completely bamboozled the computer system – another useful skill.

"Well done, Grandad."

We were soon faced with another problem. There was another reception desk at the entrance to **MARLIN SHIPPING**, manned by a blonde woman. "How will I get past her?"

The answer came quite quickly, as a cleaner passed by, pushing a trolley. "Grandad, do your blowy thing at the reception desk."

He nodded, puffed out his cheeks and blew, while I fell in behind the trolley.

A breeze blew papers up in the receptionist's face. She scrambled to pick them up. That was all the diversion I needed.

The cleaner stopped too, watching the papers fluttering about. I just kept walking. Next thing I knew I was strolling through the banks of desks in Marlin's open plan office.

"This is it," said Grandad. "Over here." He led me towards the big floor-to-ceiling window at the end. On the way, I stopped to pick up a clipboard and pen. It made me look official, like I was carrying out some sort of inspection.

"There," he said, pointing out a desk in a quiet section next to the window.

I knelt down and pretended to tie my shoelaces. Then, after a quick look about, I crept closer.

No one had seen me, and I was within touching distance of Morrison's desk. I felt a huge flush of satisfaction, as I leant over to pull open the top drawer.

That's when my head crashed into someone else's. A girl's. She was about my age, with straight brown hair and hazel eyes. And she was reaching for the same drawer.

CHAPTER 23

The Grapefruit Flamenco

"OW!" we both cried.

I clutched my head. So did she.

"Who are you?" she said in an annoyed voice.

"Well, who are you?" I deliberately made myself sound equally annoyed.

She flashed her eyes fiercely. "This is my story, so clear off!"

"Your story? What?"

She shouldered me out of the way and slid open the top drawer. The tip of her tongue poked out of the side of her mouth as she rummaged through it. I tried to rummage too, but she slapped my hand away. "Ow!"

"Clear off, I told you!" she said.

"Sshhh!" said Grandad. "Someone's coming."

I nudged her, and we both scurried under the desk and hid. Just in time too, as a pair of men's feet came strutting by.

I shut my eyes and tried to stay completely still. I dared not even breathe.

"It's OK," said Grandad after a moment. "He's gone."

I nudged the girl again, and we crawled out from under the desk.

For the first time, she looked at me. It was like she was trying to weigh me up. "Thanks," she said.

"Oh, don't thank me."

She delved into the drawer again, and dug out a clutch of memory sticks, the kind of things you plug into the side of your computer. She thumbed through them, flicking most of them back into the drawer, before settling on one in particular.

"Ah-ha!" she declared.

"What's that?"

"Evidence, I bet," said Grandad. "What is she up to?"

"Wouldn't you like to know," the girl said, winking.

I could see from the way she was dressed, with a plain, open-necked shirt and her school blazer and tie tucked over her schoolbag, that she was trying the same simple disguise as me. But why?

"Who are you?" I asked.

"Never you mind," she said, getting up and straightening her dress.

"If you're looking for Morrison, then I can help… maybe," I said.

She surveyed me through narrowed eyes, but didn't reply.

I went on: "My name's Jay Patel. I'm not doing a story, I promise."

"Then what are you doing?" she asked.

"There's a café down the street," I said. "Let me explain."

"Are you buying?"

I nodded, wondering if what pocket money I had left would be enough to afford anything.

She smiled, a broad, toothy grin. "Great! I'm Sian Hanlon, from the *St Knocker Sentinel*." And she shook my hand.

El Fruit-io was a Spanish-themed smoothie bar. All the servers were dressed up as pieces of citrus fruit. They danced to salsa music, carried maracas round with them, and wore sombreros.

Grandad stared round at the place, shaking his head in disbelief. "Do the staff get paid extra to look this daft?"

I sipped on my Orange Fiesta, mourning the loss of five whole pounds and sixty pence. This had better be worth it, I thought.

Meanwhile Sian slurped loudly on her Grapefruit Flamenco, her bicycle helmet resting on the tabletop beside her.

"What's the *St Knocker Sentinel*?" I asked. It wasn't a newspaper I'd ever heard of.

"Oh," she said. "It's my school, St Knocker's Academy. The *Sentinel* is our news blog. I've been investigating a story on illegal diamond mining around the world." She put her drink down and stared at me earnestly. "Did you know that they force kids our age to work down these mines? It's practically slave labour. They smuggle the diamonds out. No one knows exactly how. But what I do know is that one of **MARLIN SHIPPING'S** executives was arrested on suspicion of diamond smuggling. He got off with it of course; someone bribed the judge."

She took another huge slurp from her smoothie. "Thanks for the drink, by the way." She smiled.

Grandad grinned at me and put on a funny sing-song voice. "Ohhh, Jayesh Patel, taking his girlfriend out for a drink..."

He could see his taunt was annoying me, so he kept going. "Jayesh and Sian, sitting in a tree, K-I-S-S-I-N-G!"

I felt my face flush. I really wanted to tell him where

to get off, but all I could do, without looking like an idiot in front of Sian, was scrunch my face up at him when she wasn't looking.

"Anyway," she went on, "I made contact with Morrison. He said he had a huge scoop that would blow everything out of the water, and he wanted to meet. I don't think he realised the *St Knocker Sentinel* was just a school newspaper. He thought he could sell the story for loads of money. When he found out I didn't have any he sort of stormed off.

"I've been following him since. Except for the last few days. He seems to have disappeared. And I think it might be serious, because when I went to his flat, someone had already been there before me, and they'd ransacked it. They were obviously looking for something."

She opened out her palm to reveal the memory stick. A tiny sticker on the front read, in miniature letters:

PROJ. 212

"What is it?" I asked.

"PROJECT 2-1-2," she said. "It's the code name for one of the illegal diamond mines, probably the worst of them, where kids as young as seven and eight years old are forced to work. Facts, figures, money trails – I bet it's all in here. I'm going to blow this wide open." She gazed dreamily into the air and moved her hand from one side to another, as if running it along a name plaque. "Sian Hanlon – master journalist!"

Grandad chortled. "Ha! Master journalist and master detective! You and your girlfriend could be a double act: Hanlon and Patel. You better tell her about Morrison now."

I nodded. "The thing is – Morrison, he's dead."

She stopped mid-slurp. Her eyes widened in shock. I went on to tell her about the body in the library, the dead janitor and **Duke's Laundry**. Her face sickened and she pushed her smoothie aside.

"We seem to be mixed up in something big," she said.

We do, I thought, but I was more interested in clearing my mum and me of murder than ridding the world of its diamond mines. At least, for now. One thing at a time. "Is there anything you can think of that might give us a lead?" I asked. "Anyone he met? Anywhere he went? Anything he mentioned, however small?"

She considered this for a moment, and then her eyes flickered. "Yes! Maybe. There was someone. I was following him. They met in the middle of the Squinty Bridge. You know, that one with the big arch that crosses the Clyde near the Science Centre. I didn't understand at the time, but now it makes sense."

"Who was it?" I asked, but then one of the waiters interrupted.

The man was dressed as a satsuma, wearing a bullfighter's hat and playing a pair of castanets with stylish abandon. I was expecting a Spanish accent too, but when he spoke it was in broad Glaswegian. I was a bit disappointed.

"'Scuse me." He was looking at Sian. "Somebody across the street just phoned in. The polis are takin' your bike away."

"Oh, right!" Sian jumped to her feet and grabbed her bicycle helmet. "Back in a sec." She sprinted through the door and disappeared.

"Hmm, what do you think?" asked Grandad.

I was about to tell him too, but then a thought struck me. Something huge. Something that slapped me across the face like a giant wet fish jumping out of the Clyde. It sent a shiver up my spine, adrenalin pumping through my veins.

I could have been wrong. It was just a hunch. I hoped I was, but I didn't think so.

Somebody phoned in, the waiter had said. I could have kicked myself.

I raced outside, only to find Sian's bike lying on the pavement, her helmet skittering across the tarmac, and her feet being dragged into the back of a van.

"Stop!"

The van screeched off, and the doors slammed shut as it veered round the corner.

A white van.

With the words *Duke's Laundry* printed across the side.

CHAPTER 24

The Dead Ankles

My first thought was to chase after the van, but it was already out of sight. And I couldn't use Sian's bike; it was still chained up to the railings.

"They are heading back across the river," said Grandad.

"We have to get to the laundry... fast!" I said. I'd just spent most of my pocket money on comedy Spanish-style beverages, so there was no chance of a taxi. Fortunately, I had just enough for a bus ticket.

Picking up Sian's helmet, I raced to the nearest stop, and caught the first bus heading for Govanhill.

"Wait!" said the driver, a very large man with red cheeks, as I tossed my coins in the slot. "A child's fare is eighty pence."

"What?" I said. "No, it's not."

"Aye, it is," he said.

"Wait," I said. "I was on a bus yesterday and it was seventy-five pence!"

"That was yesterday," he replied. "And it's eighty pence today. Look." He pointed up at a sign, which read:

"The fares went up today."

This was a disaster. Seventy-five pence was all I had left. It meant I couldn't go anywhere. "Look, driver… sir, it's an emergency," I said.

"Yes," Grandad added, "you tell him." He leaned his head through the driver's window, and began yelling in the man's face. "You great galoot!"

The driver sniffed the air, as if he'd just picked up a bad smell.

"Was that me?" said Grandad, delighted. So delighted in fact that he started joking around. "Oh, I do apologise, it must have been that prawn vindaloo I ate the night before I died!"

Eventually a man behind me wearing a lumberjack-style jacket stepped forward, sighing deeply and shaking his head. "Here," he said, and popped five pence into the slot.

The driver nodded, satisfied, and printed off my ticket.

"One more thing!" I said to him as he issued his last bus ticket and was driving off. I rapped on his window.

"Don't talk to me, I'm driving!" he snapped.

"What if it's *really* important?" I asked.

He scoffed. "Always is."

"There's this girl. You see, she's been kidnapped. And, look I know it's hard to believe, but you have to call the police on your radio."

The driver burst out in sarcastic laughter. "Oh, I get it, ha ha!" He screwed up his nose and spoke in a weird squeaky voice, which I hoped was not an impression of me. "Make a fool of the driver, play a practical joke."

"No, really. Just radio it in, please!"

"Hu! OK, so what's her name, then?" he asked.

"Sian."

"Sian whit?"

I shrugged. "I can't remember."

"Hah! You might have done better than that. You can't even think up a good name. And where did it happen?"

"This place called *El Fruit-io*."

He burst into laughter again, this time, genuine side-splitting guffaws. "You must think I sailed up the Clyde on a tea biscuit."

"No, really, it's a smoothie bar. The guys are all dressed up as satsumas."

He laughed even harder. "I'm not falling for that. Do you know how many folk try and play jokes on me? It's no' fair. I didn't become a bus driver to get laughed at all day long you know." His face turned serious, and his cheeks were getting redder and angrier. "I became a bus driver so as I could drive buses and no' have to talk to people. See this window?" He jabbed at the glass screen between him and me. "That's a message. It says: DON'T TALK TO ME."

The man with the lumberjack coat, who had broad ox-like shoulders, barged through the other passengers, passing straight through Grandad as he did so.

Grandad crossed his eyes and gave a groan. "Watch it!"

The man grabbed me by the hood of my parka and barked at the driver, "Is this boy bothering you?"

"Aye, actually, he is," the driver replied.

"No!" cried Grandad. "He is the one being an idiot! You leave my grandson be."

"Right, that's it! Aff the bus!" growled the man.

"Get him oot!" cried a tiny sour-faced old lady in the front seat.

"Wee troublemaker! Stop the bus! Chuck him off!" moaned an old man with a round face. He reached up to press the stop button.

"Oh no you don't!" Grandad must have done it on instinct. He reached up to catch the man's wrist. Amazingly, he succeeded.

The man's eyes widened in horror as he stared at his hand, which was frozen in midair. "Wha... WHAAAAA...!"

"Did you see that?" cried Grandad. He clapped his hands and did a really cool dance – all head bobbing and arm wiggling, like in a Bollywood movie. "I can touch things! I can actually touch things!"

I did see it, but I was too busy being grappled by a lumberjack rhinoceros. The driver pulled over, the doors pistoned open, and the man pushed me out onto the pavement.

As the bus drove off, Grandad shouted after it, shaking his fist, "I *will* look for you, I *will* find you, and I WILL haunt you!"

He clasped his hands around his back and then turned to me. "That went well. So what now?"

I couldn't see a phonebox around anywhere to call the police. There was nothing else for it. "We run!" I said. "Or at least, I run, you float."

Grandad shrugged. "OK, sounds good." He seemed to have mastered the art of floating. He was faster than me now. In fact, he kept stopping to turn and complain. "Come on, I could run faster than that when I was fifty-eight!"

I was panting by the time I reached **Duke's Laundry**. I reckoned it took me twenty-one minutes and forty seconds to get there, which must've been enough to get me into the *Guinness Book of Records*. Though I don't suppose anyone has ever bothered to set a record for pelting it across half of Glasgow.

There was no sign of the van outside. I burst in, my heart thumping, ready to confront Maw Cleggan. Only no one was at the desk.

"Hello! HELLO!" I bellowed. "SIAN!"

No answer.

"I will go through and check," said Grandad, ducking through the doorway into the back.

I propped myself against the counter to get my breath back. Then I heard Grandad shouting, "JAYESH! You had better come in here!"

I dodged behind the counter into the back. I found myself in a large, well-lit hall, filled with industrial washers and dryers. None of them were being used. The place was completely quiet.

None of them, except one. A tumble dryer, a large commercial one. It had just come off a cycle; I could tell from the heat rising from it. Its door was lying open and a pair of feet were sticking out.

Chubby feet wearing luminous yellow trainers.

Maw Cleggan's luminous yellow trainers.

"She is dead!" I heard Grandad say. It was like an echo in my head, and everything seemed to be going in slow motion.

Some kind of instinct made me grab her by the ankles. I'm not sure why, maybe I was going to try and pull her out.

Just then, all the doors in the place smashed open at once.

"GO! GO! GO!"

A dozen armed police officers burst in, pointing guns with red laser sights around the room. Red lasers that swiftly focused on me.

Uniformed officers wearing high-visibility vests followed close behind them. Outside, the chop-chop-chop of a helicopter could be heard hovering overhead.

A figure in a suit stepped out from between two armed men.

It was DI Graves, managing to look both extremely grim and extremely smug at the same time.

"Well, well, Mr Patel."

"Can I help you?" Grandad and I both replied.

She jabbed her thumb towards Maw Cleggan's very dead ankles.

"That's a new one," she said. "Death by tumble dryer."

CHAPTER 25

The Ghostly Confession

Interview room seven was cold and drab, its only features being a barred window high up on the wall, and a tiny radiator in the corner.

Funnily enough, cold and drab was also how I felt at that moment, facing down DI Graves' icy stare, especially since I'd just made myself prime suspect for three different murders.

"So," she said, cracking her knuckles like she was slowly snapping the backbone of a small mammal. "Is it not about time you came clean?"

"She's right, boy," said Grandad, who was still straining to squeeze himself through the door, after DI Graves had slammed it in his face. "This has gone far enough. Let them deal with it. Tell her what you know, then you can go home."

Even I had to admit Grandad was right. I was in over my head. In the space of two days I'd somehow accumulated involvement in three murders, a kidnapping, and one or two people who wanted me dead.

"Or," said DI Graves, "would you prefer us to pin the murders on you? Cos it's easy done."

Constable McBurnie had been sitting beside her, his arms folded, looking bored, but he suddenly sat up, as if he'd been hit by a brainwave. "Oh, could we just do that? Please?"

"You leave my boy be!" cried Grandad, as he finally pulled himself out of the door with a...

POP!

He sat on the floor and sighed. "Oh, I hate doing that."

Graves shot McBurnie a scolding look, but he carried on. "I mean, I'm sick of this case now! Look, there was a big fight outside the butcher's this afternoon. They'd run out of mince. A huge rammy, it was. It was spilling out onto the streets and everything. All units got scrambled, helicopters, dogs, the anti-terrorist squad. Every police officer in Pollockshields, except me! I missed it. And where am I? Here in a room interviewin' some wee boy. I might've missed the biggest bust-up Glasgow's ever seen! All because of this stupid case."

McBurnie stopped, and there was a moment's silence while he looked at Graves, and then looked at me, and then back at her again. Graves didn't respond, she just stared straight at me, the same cold look on her face.

"Moan, moan, moan," said Grandad. "In my day police officers did not moan, they just got on with it."

Eventually McBurnie tutted and slumped back in his seat again.

"OK," I said. "What do you want to know?"

"First up, what took you to the laundry?" she said.

"I was following the white van, the one that showed up on the CCTV from the school." I leaned forward. "The CCTV you people didn't check."

Was that a tinge of redness on her cheeks, I thought? Good, she *should* be embarrassed.

"Ouch!" said Grandad. "You might have touched a nerve there."

McBurnie leaned forward and raised a finger. Another brainwave was on the way. "Could we not nick him for obstruction?"

Grandad leaned into his face. "You! Shut up!" He pursed his lips and blew in McBurnie's ear. The policeman threw up his hand. "Ow!" Then he looked around, confused.

Graves ignored all this, and so did I. I told her all about Fred and Ginger, describing them in detail. I told them about how they removed Morrison's body from the school in the rolled-up carpet.

"Big Davie saw it too. He said he would report it for me, which I thought was a good idea, seeing as you said you never wanted to hear from me or my family again."

Her cheeks reddened further, while McBurnie drummed his fingers on his chin, then pointed towards Sian's pink bicycle helmet, which sat on the table in front of me. "Hey! Have you got a licence for that bike?"

"You don't need a licence for a bike," sighed Graves.

"Oh NO?" he said dramatically.

"It's not mine," I said.

"AHAAAA!!" cried McBurnie, leaping to his feet and pointing a finger of accusation right in my face. "You NICKED it!"

"Right, that's it!" said Grandad. He steadied himself, and launched a kick at McBurnie's backside. His leg went straight through, but McBurnie yelped and jumped in the air. "What was that?"

"Sit down!" ordered Graves.

I carried on: "Someone got to Big Davie before he could report it, but I don't know how."

I also told her everything I knew about Morrison and **MARLIN SHIPPING**, where he worked. And finally – Sian. "The most important thing you need to do is find that white van."

"Why?"

"Look, I've told you about ten times – Fred and Ginger took a friend of mine, a girl my age."

"Yes, the kidnapping," she said.

"A kidnapping?" said McBurnie, suddenly excited. "At last, we're getting somewhere! Tell us more."

"I'm going to kick him again!" said Grandad. He drew

his leg back, and launched another kick, but this time McBurnie didn't react. "Oh, I can't do it! That last one took it right out of me."

I dangled the bike helmet from its strap as I told Graves all about Sian, what school she went to and how she linked in with Morrison. "She was looking into illegal diamond mining. It was called PROJECT 212. I'm not sure how it's connected to all this, but I'm sure it is, somehow."

Graves' cheeks went white this time. "Yes, that is extremely serious information," she said.

I nodded. If I was out of my depth, I was pretty sure she was wearing armbands. "Shouldn't you be doing something by now?" I asked.

Graves was tapping the end of her pen hard on the desk, like she was squashing insects with it. "Don't worry, we've put out an alert for the white van. We'll find your friend. It's our top priority." She pushed back her seat and stood up.

"Good!" declared McBurnie. "That'll give me something decent to do, instead of sitting about here like a muppet." He leaned forward, as if confiding a secret in me. "I thought this job was going to be all cop cars flying about and chasing baddies. All I seem to do is stand about, guarding things, or watching, or waiting, or fillin' in stupid forms."

"Do you still have my business card?" Graves said to me. "If you think of anything else, I mean, *anything* you forgot – call me."

She opened my palm and pressed five pound coins into it. "What's this for?" I asked.

She flung open the interview room door. "Your taxi. We're releasing you now. Both of you."

"Really? My mum too?"

"RESULT!" cried Grandad, pumping his fist.

"Oh, yes." Graves led me down the corridor to another interview room. It was one of those rooms with a two-way mirror, which meant the people outside could see in, but the people inside couldn't see out. Mum was sitting on top of the table, her legs crossed in the lotus position, and her long, flowing skirt draped all around her. Her hands were outstretched and she was chanting:

"I am fuuuull of love and peeeeeaaace!"

"I'll be glad to be rid of her, to be honest," said Graves. "She's only been here one afternoon and she's turned the place on its head. Two of my officers handed in their notice to go and become Buddhist monks. Oh, and she found a spirit path between the staff canteen and the toilets, so everyone else thinks the station is haunted."

"It IS haunted," said McBurnie.

"Oh, it definitely is." Grandad, gritted his teeth and pulled his leg back to kick McBurnie, but once again there was no reaction. "Ach! I've lost it! I'm too tired."

Graves caught my arm. "And, please, don't get any more involved in this matter."

The edges of her mouth turned up slightly. It wasn't exactly what you'd call a smile, but it was at least some way from being a frown. And then she was gone, shuttling down the corridor with McBurnie in her wake, who was suddenly keen as mustard now he knew there was a chase on.

"You heard the woman," said Grandad. "Don't get any more involved in this matter. That is good advice."

Good advice, yes. I had to agree. Except *this matter* was still involved with *me*.

CHAPTER 26

The Rissole Escape

Mum stayed sitting in the lotus position in the back seat of the taxi home. And now she was chanting:

"I am caaallm and at peeeaaaace!"

That is, until the taxi driver leaned round and said, "Do ye mind knocking that off?" He glared at us. "And could ye get your Dr. Martens off my seat n'all?"

Suddenly Mum lapsed out of her trance. Her face twisted up into a snarl and she barked back at him, "Shuttup, ya muppet! And drive!"

Mum unwrapped her legs, then placed her right foot on top of her left knee. She clasped her hands together, closed her eyes, and then, instead of chanting she began to hum, which was almost as annoying.

"I'm so sorry you were dragged into all this, dearie," she said to me, between hums.

She assumed the police only interviewed me because of her. Surely even Mum must have wondered why her son was found in the back of a laundry with the dead body of a Glasgow crime lord. Or rather, in Maw Cleggan's case, crime lady, or even more appropriate, crime gorilla.

She continued, "Don't think I don't know what's going on here. I do."

"You do?" Or was I wrong about Mum? Maybe she did know. For a second I thought I was about to be rumbled. That is, until she leaned towards me and spoke, her eyes glistening with concern. "Your aura, it's damaged."

"My what?"

"Your aura, the field of energy surrounding your body. It's too mauve!" She flung her hands up to her cheeks, as if it was a big disaster.

Grandad groaned and passed his hand over his face. "Here she goes! My son married a fruitcake!"

"Right," I said. "Mauve, and that's bad?"

"Mauve means danger."

"Ha!" laughed Grandad. "Well, she's right about that. You have been in danger." He sighed. "I feel bad, boy. I know you are trying to find your father, but you should not be doing it alone. Your mother lives in a fantasy world. As for your granny, she is too old and frail."

"Ha!" Now it was my turn to burst out laughing. "Frail? Have you ever seen Granny hack down a wall with a claw hammer?" The older Granny got the more she seemed like a kind of robot terminator, on a secret mission to rip things apart.

"Oh, I would love to see that," grinned Grandad.

"What did you say?" asked Mum, with a look of mild amusement. I'd forgotten once again that I was having two separate conversations at once.

"Eh, nothing Mum, just talking to myself."

"Quite right, dearie," said Mum. "I do that all the time too."

When we got back to the flat Granny was in the hall. One of the bedroom doors was off, and she was bent double over a workbench, sanding the door with a look of ferocious glee.

Mum got dinner ready while I went to my bedroom, slumped down on the bed and stared at the wall. Stared at the leads to Dad's disappearance, marked out and criss-crossed in string over the map of Glasgow. Leads that, so far, had got me nowhere.

At times like this I really missed my dad. He would've given me a big bear hug, as he always did, hoisting me off my feet, spinning me round, before collapsing on the bed in hysterics.

I shook my head. I couldn't think like this. I had to pull myself together and focus on the case. I started running through everything that had happened in my mind. I turned over Morrison's business card in my fingers.

James Morrison
Sales Executive

MARLIN SHIPPING AGENTS

Tel
0141 6783452

Email
James@marlinshipping.co.uk

Website
www.marlinshipping.co.uk

I reached into my schoolbag and yanked out a copy of the school handbook, then flicked through it. Cheap paper, loads of errors. Then the price list I picked up from *Duke's Laundry*. The same cheap paper, and the same errors. The price list was practically gobbledygook. It barely made any sense at all, as if it had been written by a senile computer. Or someone who really couldn't be bothered... who didn't want customers.

I went in to the kitchen, wrinkled up my nose at the smell of Mum's cooking, flipped open the laptop and checked out *Big A Printers*.

"I see you are not going to let this go, are you?" said Grandad.

He was right. I was weighing up whether or not I really could stay out of this. Not because I wanted to find the murderer myself. I was happy to let the police do all of that now. It was because of Sian. She'd been kidnapped, and finding her was a race against time. And let's face it, the Pollockshields police force had not exactly covered themselves in glory so far.

A loud reverberating gong called me and Granny to the dinner table. Which would have been fine, except I was already sitting there. My eardrums rattled.

Mum set the plates down in front of us with a flourish. "Ta-daaaaaaa. Spicy nut rissoles." She announced it as if it was the next act at a cabaret – the worst, most depressing cabaret ever.

Squirrel vomit. *Burnt* squirrel vomit.

Even Granny looked defeated.

Grandad puffed out his cheeks. "Never thought I would say this, but for once I am glad to be dead."

Both Granny and me pretended to eat, which mainly involved rearranging our food around the plate. I began to wish we had a cat, just so that I could feed this rubbish to it, though it would have to be a pretty weird squirrelly kind of cat that enjoyed punishment. Granny waited until Mum wasn't looking and scraped her plate into a plant pot, which was a shame, because that's exactly where I was planning to put it, and there wasn't any room now.

Fortunately, Granny was looking out for me. She quickly emptied mine into her toolbox and slipped me a five-pound note under the table, then nodded towards the front door.

Now all I needed was a diversion, so I could slip out of

the house unnoticed. It wasn't long in coming, as Mum's 'Earth Healing' group soon arrived for their weekly meeting. This was a bunch of people just like her, who spent an evening a week carrying out the vital work of putting the world back together, all with the power of their positive mind waves.

The hall was soon full of them, dressed up in what looked like old curtains, with leggings underneath, wearing bandanas, and dancing round in a circle singing, "*All you need is love...*"

Meanwhile, Granny had gone back to her DIY, and was lying on her side on the floor, a tin of white paint by her side, daubing the skirting boards.

"It's like Central Station in here," said Grandad.

"Follow me." I grabbed my parka and slipped out the door.

Fifteen minutes later, I stood in the queue at the local fast-food restaurant, fingering the five-pound note Granny had given me. All around me was bustle and noise, from the servers behind the counters rushing about fetching chips and drinks, to the close press of people behind me in the queue. Yet I felt detached from it all. I suppose I should have felt a sense of relief, a great weight lifted off my shoulders. It was all up to the police now, and I could go back to my life. But part of me just couldn't. I kept worrying about Sian. I hoped she was alright.

More than anything, I was tired, and I hadn't eaten all day, apart from a few pretend bites of Mum's squirrel rissole.

"Oh, man!" said Grandad, who was standing off to one side. "Do I miss chicken burgers!"

Someone dropped a load of coins at my feet, just as I was picking up my tray. Then a massive scrum of people bent down to help pick them up.

I flopped down at a booth in the quietest part of the restaurant. I slurped my drink and prised open the box, only to find my appetite desert me. I kept turning over the deaths in my mind. I was thinking about what linked Morrison to the school. And Maw Cleggan, for that matter. That link was the epicentre of this whole thing. That missing link was what led to them both being murdered.

Grandad plonked himself on the seat opposite. He nodded down at my burger, as if offended. "Are you not eating that? I hate to see good food go to waste." He licked his ghostly lips together. "Oh, being dead is rubbish!"

I touched my fingers to the bridge of my nose. There was a throbbing pain in my head that was building, and I felt woozy. A strange feeling. A strange, sleepy feeling, an urge to close my eyes and sink into a dark hole. It was almost as if I'd been...

"Jayesh?" he asked. "Are you OK, boy?"

Grandad's voice echoed round my head. Then a man slumped down on top of him. A man I recognised from somewhere. A brown raincoat and fedora hat. Up close, his skin was dark, rough and blotchy. He grinned. A wide smile, white teeth. "Hello."

"OW!" said Grandad, moving over. "Do you have any idea how much that hurts a ghost? I mean, hurts its feelings? It's like I'm not here at all." Which he wasn't, to be fair. "Nice hat, though!"

I felt my eyes drooping now. As hard as I tried, I just couldn't keep them open. I thought back to when I was standing at the counter with my tray. The dropped coins. I remembered a hand reaching over my tray just as everyone bent down to look. That was when it must have happened.

I'd been drugged.

"Jayesh?" said Grandad, as my head lolled forward. The man in the overcoat reached out his hands to catch me.

CHAPTER 27

The Tongs Torture

When I opened my eyes again, groggy and dry-mouthed, I found myself staring at the same man.

Except something was different. For a start, he wasn't wearing his overcoat and hat any more. They were hanging up on a solitary coat stand in the corner behind him. Underneath he wore a grey waistcoat and trousers, with a white open-necked shirt, and his sleeves rolled up. I noticed he had perfect nails and neatly styled black hair, which was shaved in at the sides and swept over on top.

I wasn't in the fast food restaurant any more either. I was in some kind of factory space, with a bare concrete floor, breezeblock walls, a corrugated steel roof, and a door at either end.

"Jayesh!" It was Grandad's voice. "Are you OK, boy?" His ghostly face loomed into mine. As if being pale and greenish wasn't bad enough, it now took on a creased, worried look.

The only response I could give was to cough. My throat ached. It felt like someone had driven a truck down it.

The man was slouched back on a chair opposite, one ankle balanced on his knee, picking his teeth with his fingernail. "Nice burger, by the way," he said.

"That guy ate your burger and kidnapped you!" said Grandad, indignant. "Better than letting it go to waste, I suppose. But still..."

"Water," I croaked.

"Give him water!" Grandad demanded, pointing out a plastic water bottle sitting at the man's feet. "Are you heartless? You drug him, you kidnap him, and you don't even give him anything to drink! He is my grandson!"

"Please, don't worry," said the man. He had a trace of an accent, but what was it? Spanish? No, maybe Portuguese. "I will give you the water. In a while. I might even let you go. It depends."

"On what?" I asked.

"On whether you co-operate."

"Huh! I'll get you the water!" declared Grandad. "Just you wait. I'm going to lift the bottle." He bent over, wrapped his greenish hands around it, and gritted his teeth. "I've got this! I've got this!" He heaved and strained. The bottle wobbled slightly. I thought for a second he really was going to lift it. But then it just tipped up and fell over onto the floor. "I have not got this yet!" Grandad said, disappointed.

The man merely glanced down at it, puzzled, then shrugged, and continued picking his teeth for a bit.

"Mind if I ask where I am?" I croaked.

He looked round at the place. "I rented this facility. It is very reasonable."

"You are in an industrial unit," said Grandad. "That one right next door to the tennis centre, you know." I pictured it in my head. I'd gone past it a few times. It wasn't far from school. I started working out an escape plan in my head, but Grandad was already on it. "You are upstairs. That door behind him is the way out. It's just on a snib, so it is easy to open. And look..." He nodded down at my hands. They were free. The man hadn't tied me up. What did that say? It told me he was pretty confident, perhaps too confident for his own good.

"And who are you?" I asked.

He shrugged. "It's no problem. I can tell you. My name is Valente. Hector Valente. I represent the G.D.F."

I was surprised when he told me his name. Not many kidnappers would. And who he worked for. And even more surprised when he flicked his business card at me. My pockets were getting stuffed with these things.

I turned it over.

GLOBAL DIAMOND FEDERATION   WEBSITE: GDF.ORG
123 RUA GRANDE, LISBON

HECTOR VALENTE
VICE PRESIDENT

TEL: +351 21 9873416   EMAIL: THESTYLIST@GDF.ORG

It gave his office address as Lisbon. So, I was right about him being Portuguese. "G.D.F. is short for Global Diamond Federation."

Diamonds!!!

I imagined some tiny diamonds floating individually around a lady's neck. "G.D.F. – never heard of it, but it sounds important," I said.

"We are a consortium of diamond exporters, who have a legitimate interest in what happens to our diamonds."

Morrison, **MARLIN SHIPPING**, diamond mines, PROJECT 212; now the diamonds round the lady's neck were beginning to link together, one by one, piece by piece.

"So, let me ask you," he continued, and his face turned into a fierce snarl.

"WHERE ARE OUR DIAMONDS?"

"HE. DOES. NOT. KNOW!" yelled Grandad.

"You're probably expecting me to say this," I said, "but I really don't know."

Valente gave a self-satisfied chortle. "Yes, indeed. But, you'll talk."

He stood up, strolled over to a table and unrolled a large bundle of cloth. I caught a collective glimmering of cold steel: sharpened blades, tongs and weird tubes.

"No!" cried Grandad.

I gulped.

"Oh, you'll talk," said Valente. "You see…" He picked up the tiniest bit of his torture kit, which looked like a metallic comb, and began ambling over to me. My skin crawled. "We knew someone was smuggling these diamonds back from Africa. We just didn't know how."

Africa, I thought.

Of course, that was where PROJECT 212 and the diamond mines were located. Now the chain was linking up, right round the lady's neck. Back to where it all began.

He waggled the comb in my face. "You are involved in this. You are the one who keeps showing up. You are the one the police are interested in. Now, come on."

"Please," I said, "I'm only mixed up in it because my mum found a body in the library. But the body disappeared. And then my friend Davie and me saw the white van on CCTV taking the body away, but he got killed… eh… and that took me to **Duke's Laundry** and Maw Cleggan, but now she's dead too… And Morrison took us to **MARLIN SHIPPING**, where we met this girl Sian, but she got kidnapped, so now she's also gone… Uh, this doesn't sound good, does it?"

Valente was staring at me side-on, as if he was sizing me up for a portrait. A cold chill crept up my spine as he stepped closer.

"What are you going to do to me?" I asked.

"Do not touch him!" cried Grandad. "If you touch him I will haunt you! I mean it!" He looked about, frantic. Then he looked down at his hands, angled himself and launched

a kick at Valente's backside. Grandad's foot went right through and Valente barely noticed. "Ahhh! It's useless being a ghost!"

Well, he could reliably sneeze and blow up a fine gust of wind, so that was something. But Valente was pretty strong. I didn't imagine a blast of air would shift that thing from his fingers, or put him off what he was about to do. I thought of punching him in the stomach and making a run for it. That would at least give me a fighting chance. But it would probably just make him angry.

And then he took something else from his back pocket, something shiny and sharp.

The Fringe Evasion

"What am I going to do to you?" He waved a pair of scissors in my face. "Why, I'm going to cut your hair, of course."

"Eh?" I said.

"EH?" said Grandad.

He suddenly began brushing my hair with the comb, and trimming bits off with the scissors. Snipping swiftly and efficiently, like a good barber. He was humming and whistling while he did it. "Aside from being an agent for the G.D.F., I am also one of Lisbon's top hairdressers," he said. "I'm sorry, but people in this country have such bad hair. Don't worry, I'm going to fix things for you, and then we're going to talk."

I glanced round at the table. Those shiny, steely objects in the unrolled bundle were all pieces of hairdressing equipment: combs, scissors, razors, that kind of thing.

Meanwhile, Grandad had squeezed himself through one of the doors, the one behind me. "OUCH! I hate that!"

I wondered what he was up to. He'd have a job of running for help, as nobody else could see him but me. Then I heard a noise, a long, spine-tingling wail, which rose up from the other side of the door and echoed off the metallic roof.

"AAAIIIIEEEE!"

Even I had to admit, it sounded quite frightening. As for Valente, he froze. His eyes gaped at the door.

"Excuse me one second," he said, and stepped gingerly towards it. His hand reached up and gripped the handle, turned it. The door creaked open.

A sudden gust of air caught the door and blew it wide. It slammed against the wall. Valente tumbled onto his back with a kind of whimper. And there was Grandad, standing at the open doorway, puffing his cheeks.

He paused for a second and glared at me. "Run, boy!"

I didn't need a second invitation. I sprinted for the other door. All hope rested on being able to open it. I fiddled with the snib. For a split second I thought it was stuck. My hands were shaking, blood was rushing in my ears.

Then it suddenly flicked up, and I turned the knob and flung the door open.

A set of stone steps led downwards. I took them three at a time. At the bottom was a fire exit. I glanced over my shoulder to see Valente stagger through the doorway. Grandad was floating in front of him, blowing in his face.

"What? STOP!" cried Valente.

Outside was a dark alleyway. I couldn't see an escape route on either side. The last thing I wanted to do was run down a dead end. But there was a fence. Tall, but easily climbable.

I hauled myself over, just as Valente appeared at the fire exit behind me.

"Come back, fella!" he yelled. "I haven't even done your fringe yet!"

I ran along a chain link fence, then through an opening. Suddenly my eyes were dazzled by bright light shining from above. Floodlights. They must have been movement-sensitive ones, for the tennis players, as I was standing on a tennis court. More than one tennis court in fact. There were about eight of them, stretched out ahead of me in two rows.

I stumbled towards an opening on the other side, passing by a long covered recess that ran the length of the place. The fence behind me rattled as Valente began climbing over it. Grandad floated across the court, shouting: "Run, Jayesh! Run!"

I tripped over something: a cable, a socket, I don't know. I clattered to the ground, before pulling myself to my feet. Then I heard a loud **PONG** from near my head, somewhere in the dark and shady recess. Something round, yellow and travelling at great speed whizzed past me and landed on the other side of the court with a **POCK**.

A tennis ball.

And another **PONG**

And another **PONG, PONG**

POCK... POCK, POCK

All at once balls were firing out from all over the place. A whole line of tennis-ball machines shooting away. It was like an artillery barrage. I must have set off something as I tripped.

Keeping low, I darted across their path.

"He's gaining on you!" cried Grandad.

Sure enough, Valente was racing closer. He was nimble, dodging the tennis balls like a boxer evading an opponent's punches. And fast. Too fast for me, I could see that. I would not be able to outrun this man.

"Ha!" he laughed, as he danced around the flying yellow

balls. He looked like he was doing the tango. "This is why in my business they call me 'The Stylist'."

Maybe in Lisbon, I thought, but this was Glasgow. We had ways of defeating anything that approached 'style'. I spotted a tennis racket lying half-in, half-out of the shadows. A cheap one, and busted too, with some of its strings gone. Someone had probably just abandoned it there. It was a gift for me. I bent down and snatched it up without breaking my stride. I turned, just as another ball launched in my direction.

PONG

I'd never learnt tennis. Didn't know the rules. Had no idea how to play. But being from Pollockshields I was good at hitting stuff. I leapt into the air. The whole world spun into slow motion as I swung the racket, smashed it hard against the ball, and aimed it square at Valente's face.

He didn't even see it coming. He was too busy shimmying around like he was on a dance floor. It whacked him straight between the eyes.

POCK

His head bounced back and he tripped, tumbling into a very unstylish heap.

Grandad laughed: "That is game, set and match to you, boy!"

It was all I needed to escape. I made for the open gate. Once through it, there were two ways I could go. One way led up to a portacabin, which served as the tennis club. The other way led across a grass pitch ringed by thick bushes and trees, and more darkness. Darkness I promptly disappeared into.

CHAPTER 29

The Bum Confrontation

Home again, and if I was expecting Mum to be waiting for me at the door, brow creased, arms folded and angrily tapping her feet, I'd have been very wrong. She hadn't even noticed I was gone.

In fact, the meeting of her 'Earth Healing' group was just reaching its final, horrific conclusion. As I walked into the hall a semi-circle of legging-clad bums confronted me, all slowly lifting up and down. Serene music was playing, and a man's voice, airy and calm, was calling out, probably from one of the bums, but from which one I couldn't tell:

"Imagine yourself floating above the Earth, high up in the atmosphere, being buffeted by gentle breezes."

Grandad chortled, pointing at one of the bums. "You would get more than buffeted by wind coming out of that."

"JAY!" cried Mum's voice. Her face, upside down, peered out from between two lemon-coloured thighs. "You must try this some time, it's exhilarating."

"It looks it, Mum," I replied. "But no thanks, I've got homework." That wasn't even half true. I'd rather do *someone else's* homework than stick my bum in the air and be buffeted.

As for Granny, she was still painting. Actually, she was painting around them, and I mean literally. Her arm was poking out from beneath someone's bum cheeks. Her hand, spotted with white and clutching a paintbrush, was carefully daubing the skirting boards.

"Oh, have you had your hair done?" said Mum. "It's nice."

Grandad guffawed and pointed to my forehead. I took a glance at myself in the hall mirror. I looked ridiculous. Valente had trimmed half my head, which left the other half untrimmed. He'd also combed down my hair in preparation to cut my fringe, but hadn't got around to it before I escaped. I tried to brush the fringe back up, but it just made me look worse. Like I'd been attacked by a crazed pair of garden shears.

"Ooooh, haven't you grown, Jay," said one of the bums. Again, not sure which.

"You're turning into a handsome young man," said another.

"Well, you are looking at him the wrong way up," said Grandad.

I smiled and nodded, then pushed my way through. As I closed my bedroom door behind me the bums were still talking to each other. In fact, one of them seemed to turn to the other as they talked. "What a shame for the boy... Must be hard for him without his dad."

I was too tired, at that point, to even think about Dad. It had been a long and exhausting day, complete with several dressings down from the police, dead bodies, kidnappings, getting drugged, and having my hair assaulted by a Portuguese special agent.

I kept thinking of that diamond necklace, those tiny little studs linking up together in a chain. Africa, the laundry, and the worst printers in the world. The pieces were coming together, but I'd have to prove it for anybody to listen.

And prove it I would, for in the dying embers of my mind that night, something was forming...

A plan.

CHAPTER 30

The Lunchtime Plan

"What are we going to do?" Grandad kept asking after I got up the next morning.

I could've explained, but where was the fun in that? I didn't have many pleasures these days, but one of them was seeing the growing look of confusion on Grandad's face.

"You'll see," I said.

"See what?" he asked, shaking his hands at me. "You need to work on your communication, boy."

I reckoned I'd string Grandad along for a while yet. "You'll find out soon."

Mum was working in the library all day so she gave us a lift to school. We left Granny behind, assaulting a flat-pack cabinet with her screwdriver.

All eyes turned to me as I entered the classroom. "Look, Jay's back!" My classmates clamoured to find out why the police had wanted to interview me the day before, and where I'd been the following afternoon.

"You should be arrested for your bad hairdo," joked Anton.

Pyotr burst out laughing.

Mwahahahaha teeheehee!!!

But only because a bear got stuck up a tree in the video he was watching on his tablet under the desk.

"Don't you listen to them, boy," said Grandad. "Yes, you do have bad hair, but tomorrow you can get it cut, and he," he pointed at Anton. "He will always be ugly."

Grandad bent over, gritted his teeth and began trying to lift Anton's pencil case into the air. To my surprise, it did budge slightly, before dropping back down. "Ha! I did it again!"

Anton looked around, slightly scared. "What! What was that?"

Freaking out my mortal enemy, Anton, was about as useful as Grandad got that morning. The rest of it he spent interrupting my learning. The worst part was when we went to the gym for a P.E. lesson. He kept marching up and down beside me while I was doing warm-ups, shouting, "Left, right, left, right, left, right!"

It was lunchtime before I was able to put my plan into gear properly.

"Follow me," I said, leading him towards the library, which was next door to the school office.

Just outside the library door, I heard a squeak and saw the door of the office opening. Two people stepped out.

I heard the voices of Mr Kessock and Mrs Cravat. I ducked back round the corner. Since my mum worked in the library I could always explain why I was there, but still, I'd rather they didn't see me here.

Mr Kessock was flapping, as usual. "All these visits from the police, what's going on? I mean, how am I supposed to win Head Teacher of the Year with all this investigating going on? It is ruining my reputation!"

Mrs Cravat seemed to take in a sharp breath, as if this was the umpteenth time today she'd had to hear this. Then she collected herself, and replied calmly. "I am sure the police have finished their investigations, and you have nothing to worry about."

"You really think so?" whined Mr Kessock.

"It's OK," said Grandad. "They're heading in the other direction."

I poked my head out. They were carrying their lunchboxes, pushing through the double doors at the other end of the corridor and heading for the staff room. That was good. That was exactly what I was banking on.

I found Mum in the library, leaning over Mrs McCleary, who was lying on her front across one of the big tables. Mum's stance reminded me of when she performed as an assistant in Dad's magician's act. She was waving her hands about in the space above Mrs McCleary's ample rear end.

"What are you doing?" I asked.

"Fixing Mrs McCleary's sciatica," Mum replied.

"By wiggling your hands over her bum?"

"Oh dearie," Mum replied, shaking her head at me as if I was simple, "I'm using my positive mental energy to heal her lower back."

Grandad chortled and leaned over to whisper in Mrs McCleary's ear, "I hope your bum gets better soon, Madam."

Mrs McCleary snored loudly in response, her head lolling to one side. "Ha! She's asleep," said Grandad. That was good too. Another potential witness out of the way.

"Now be quiet. I have to concentrate," said Mum, and she went back to jiggling her hands above Mrs McCleary's bottom.

Perfect, I thought. When Mum was doing anything like this she fell into what she called a 'state of meditation'. Sometimes the pupils in her eyes would roll up and her tongue would stick out, which was pretty weird. Whether it was a load of old rubbish or not is beside the point. It meant she was totally wrapped up in what she was doing and didn't notice as I slipped my hand into her bag and nicked her set of keys.

A large bookcase screened the connecting door to the office from Mum and her boss. I whispered to Grandad, "Nip into the office and check if the coast is clear."

He nodded, and took a deep breath, before pushing through the door, groaning. "Uurgh! I HATE that!"

He was gone for what seemed like ages. I grunted and stared at my watch. Where was he, and what did he think he was doing? I only had a short space of time, maybe fifteen minutes, to put my plan into operation. I was almost at the end of my patience when he poked his head back through the door, smiling.

"Sorry, but those Mumbari lads can really talk. You know, they are not too bad once you get past the poppy-out eyeballs and the missing limbs."

"Look, is the coast clear or not?"

"Oh, yeah, sorry, I should have told you before – there is no one in the office. No one alive, anyway."

"Yeesh!" I discreetly unlocked the connecting door to the office and slipped through.

CHAPTER 31

The Spaghetti Map

"Are you sure you know what you are doing?" Grandad said as he watched me lift the African tribal mask off the wall.

I shrugged. "Don't worry." Although I had to admit I wasn't sure. How could you ever be sure? There were so many ifs and buts. Even the great detectives, in the middle of their summing up, with all the suspects sat around them, were never a hundred percent sure. Sometimes all you had to go on were hunches and probables. This was probably even more than probable. This was a 'likely'. "I know it was stolen. That's why the Mumbari are so unhappy."

"Of course it was stolen," said Grandad, shifting about like he was being jostled on a football pitch. "These guys are the ancestors of the tribe. They want to know what your game is."

"They need to trust me," I said. "Tell them, I'll make sure the mask is sent back to Africa once this is done."

"You bet it will!" chimed in Grandad. "And it is the only thing stopping them from lynching me right now."

I settled the mask on the floor and flipped it round

so I was staring at the back. A wide, curved rim circled the edge. I ran my fingers along the inside, and stopped.

"A-ha!" I shot Grandad a meaningful look, which was completely wasted as he just stared back at me, confused. I delved further underneath the rim, then, as my fingers gripped on something soft but bumpy, I pulled. A tearing of tape, and I ripped something free – a long, thin white bag, with the duct tape still attached to it.

"A-haaaa!" I stared at it, turned it over, and yanked off the rest of the tape. I undid the top of the bag and tapped it gently.

A trio of sparkling clear stones dropped onto my palm.

Diamonds.

Rough, uncut diamonds.

For a moment, I could barely speak. Neither could Grandad. He blinked, showing me, for a moment, a whole host of faces, the ghoulish faces of the Mumbari, staring down at my hand. Everyone was entranced by the glistening rocks sitting in my palm.

Grandad blinked them away again, then whistled. "Jackpot." I carefully tipped the diamonds back into the bag. "What now then, genius?" he asked.

"Can you ask the Mumbari about that?" I pointed to the empty rack underneath where the mask hung on the wall. "Was that for some kind of ceremonial stave?"

"A what?" he asked.

"It's like a big, carved wooden stick."

"Yes," said Grandad. "They are all nodding yes. In fact,

one of them has nodded so much the top of his head has fallen off. It is pretty gross."

"A-haaaaa!" I said.

"A-haaaaa what?" said Grandad.

"That's the murder weapon. Well, for Morrison, that is. That's what the murderer used. We need to find that stave."

Something else occurred to me. I turned to the computer on the desk, which was unlocked, while Grandad spoke to the deceased tribesmen. I opened the web browser and looked up the website for *Big A Printers*.

Something I saw on there before had been playing on my mind. An out-of-hours number was listed, for 'VIP customers only': 0141 5550212. **212!**

I then checked the website for Companies House, an

organisation that holds lots of information on businesses, and, more importantly, who runs them. I wanted to find out who ran *Big A Printers* - the name of the person in charge.

And there it was.

The solution to all this was right there, in that name.

Suddenly all the clues came rushing out of my head at once, and the tiny pieces of diamond linked up together. The chain was complete. I snatched a piece of paper and scribbled everything down, like this:

"Ha!" I waved the piece of paper in Grandad's face.

"It looks like a plate of spaghetti," he said. "I hate spaghetti."

"That's the inner workings of my mind."

"Well that explains a lot. So what do we do now?"

"First, I need…" I frantically looked around the office, rooting about in cupboards and drawers.

"You need…? Your head examined?" said Grandad.

At last, I found what I was looking for. I whipped open a large plastic bag with a flourish. "I need to hide the mask." I slipped the bag over the mask so that most of it was covered. I used a smaller bag to hide the top. "Perfect," I said. "Second, we need to get it out of here. I need to disappear out of this office, out of the school. And you and the Mumbari are going to help me."

Grandad nodded. "That we can do."

CHAPTER 32

The Bus Trip

After sneaking back into the library and slipping my mum's keys back into her bag, I returned to the office and left by the office door. Grandad and the Mumbari scouted out my exit from the school, making sure I wasn't seen by anybody as I left with the mask.

I flagged down the next bus heading into town.

There were only about three people on it, and two of them were asleep. Grandad slumped down beside me on the back seat of the lower deck. He didn't say a word, he was just watching.

"You're quiet," I said.

He didn't reply, he just blinked, showing me what the Mumbari were up to. There were about twenty of them crammed into the lower deck, some of them missing arms, some missing legs, some missing their heads. It seemed they thought they were on some kind of day trip. They were all babbling excitedly. In fact, I'd never seen people so excited by a ride on a Glaswegian bus before. They were gazing around in wonder, and gesticulating in amazement at things like the luggage rack and the ticket dispenser and even the disabled seat that flipped up and down.

A few had gone upstairs to see what the top deck looked like. They now beckoned down to their colleagues, who all rushed up in a great, ghostly, swirling spiral, sucking in the air as they went.

"Any chance you could get them to go back inside the mask for a bit?" I asked.

He puffed his cheeks out. "I will try, but I am not promising anything."

When we reached the Clyde I pressed the stop button and we all got off – me, my ghost grandad and the horde of dead African tribesmen.

The river was glistening in the bright afternoon sun. I sat on a bench and pulled back the edges of the plastic bag, pointing as politely as I could towards the mask's wide grinning mouth. It took ages for Grandad to persuade them to get back in. One of them spotted a kebab shop and they all wanted to go and have a look at it. Eventually, after being allowed to see the wonders of the rotating spit, and witness as someone ordered a doner kebab and then ate it, they all whizzed up in a great swooshing circle and disappeared into the mouth of the mask.

"Phew!" I said.

"What now?" asked Grandad.

"Next," I said, "I need to make a phone call."

I strolled over to a payphone, picked up the handset and dialled a number.

Specifically, the number for *Big A Printers*. I had a hunch that someone important might answer it, partly as the number ended in **212**, and partly because by now someone back at school would have discovered the missing mask, and word would have got out. I was betting the person who answered the line was key to the investigation and that *Big A Printers* had very little to do with printing.

It rang a few times, before an answerphone message kicked in. That was a tiny bit disappointing, as I was hoping for a human voice, maybe even the voice of the person who caused all this.

"Hello," I said, after the bleep, "it's Jay Patel here. I have something you want. And you have something I want too..."

The Squinty Bridge

A few hours later I was standing in the middle of a bridge across the river, with the African tribal mask stuffed under my arm.

They call it the Squinty Bridge. I'm not sure why, though squinty was a good word to describe how I was feeling after all I'd been through in the last few days.

The bridge was busy, both with people and traffic. Blocks of designer flats and hotels surrounded it on either side, and, slightly further away, the armadillo-like hulk of the Exhibition Centre and needle-like tower of the Science Centre dominated the landscape. A mild breeze blew up the river, bringing with it spits and spots of Atlantic rain.

"I do not like this," said Grandad, eyeing the steel arch that curved overhead. "I am not sure this was a good idea. Why didn't you call the police earlier? You could have let them deal with this."

I'd telephoned Graves only ten minutes before I got here. But there was a good reason why: "They wouldn't approve of me doing this."

And I wasn't wrong. DI Graves had nearly flipped after

I told her my plan. I'm not sure she was all that bothered about me putting myself at risk, but she was more than bothered about losing the diamonds. And all she was going to get in return was yet another interfering child.

"SO?" said Grandad.

"So, this swap is the only way of saving Sian. The bad guys get their diamonds back, and we get her. Only..." I checked my watch, "as long as Graves arrives on time then the bad guys will not be making a getaway. And it is game, set and match to us."

Still, I had to give Graves her due. Once she realised that I was determined to go ahead with my plan she warmed to it. She made a few calls. As soon as the swap was made and me and Sian were safe, the cop cars would all come swarming out of the side streets and seal off the escape. At least, that was the plan.

I shrugged. "I think it's a good plan. I think my plan is going to work." I was more nervous than I seemed, but it felt good to have so many police on the way. What could possibly go wrong? They do say pride comes before a fall, and I was about to have a bit of a big one.

A vehicle drew to a halt at the north end of the bridge, facing towards us. It flashed its headlights.

"That'll be it," I said.

"I will go ahead and check it out," said Grandad, and he floated ahead of me. As I walked slowly in the direction of the van, a hooded figure got out of the passenger-side door and stood facing me, legs apart.

It wasn't until I got quite close that I saw who the figure was, and it wasn't who I thought it was going to be. That freckled face, ginger hair poking out, and the eyes, too close together. Eyes that gleamed with menace. He drew back his hood to reveal the beanie hat. It was Ginger.

"You've got something we want," he growled.

Grandad's ghostly form erupted from the side door of the van.

"OUCH!"

"I hate that!" He flapped at me. "Jayesh! She's not here! There's no Sian!"

I froze, wondering what was happening. If they'd tricked me, then why? What was their game?

Grandad pointed behind my shoulder, shouting, "LOOK OUT!"

I turned, only to find Ginger's friend, Fred, breathing down my neck.

"Aye, we've got a wee something for you," he sneered. "But first, you've to take a wee trip down the Clyde with us."

"I... what?"

Before I knew it, the men grabbed me. They swiped

the mask from under my arms, then hoisted me in the air and launched me over the side of the bridge. Ginger snarled as I fell: "Your friends aren't watching the river, are they?"

What happened next was a blur. The pounding of my heart as I tumbled, the whirling city, the freezing cold smash of the water hitting my face. A horrible thought… of plummeting into the dark depths… coming to rest on the muddy riverbed, in between the rusting hulks of old ships and discarded shopping trolleys.

Then, a pair of hands grabbing me under the shoulders, yanking me from the water and dumping me on the floor of a speedboat. A gun, an actual gun, poking in my face. Me, shivering, barely able to talk, my clothes dripping wet.

And finally, to cap it all off, a dull whack across my head. Blinding lights, and falling. A boat engine roaring to life, and the rush of water.

My brilliant plan wasn't going brilliantly well.

CHAPTER 34

The Crane Revelation

By the time I came to my senses, day had turned to night, and the mild breeze blowing in off the ocean was less than mild. It was very cold indeed. At least it was to me, soaked as I was to the skin, and shivering. My head ached, my jaw ached, every part of me ached. And that wasn't the worst part of my situation.

I jerked my wrist, only to find both hands were lashed to a rusty railing. But there was something worse. I gazed down to find I was slumped on a metal walkway grill. I could see lights below it, streetlights. Far below, a hundred metres maybe. And what did that mean?

"Jayesh! Are you OK?" It was Grandad, his pale, worried face peering into mine. "I thought I had lost you there, boy."

"I'm OK," I coughed.

"Good, I'm glad," said another voice. I felt a tug on my arm. It was Sian, who was tied up next to me.

"Oh, you're alive," I said. That was a positive at least.

"The night is young," she replied, watching a set of figures emerge from the darkness.

I recognised two of them straight away. One tall and thin, the other short and fat, both wearing beanies. They hung back, on the other side of a wide gap. A worryingly wide gap, with only very low railings blocking a sheer drop to the ground.

"Stay back, boys," came the voice of the third figure, who stepped into the amber half-light from the city below.

In that one moment, all my theories were proven right. That person was the architect of all this: a diamond smuggler, a murderer – a TRIPLE murderer. And she hadn't even started on me and Sian yet.

"Hello, Mrs Cravat," I said.

Mrs Cravat's eyes were cold and steely now. I'd never noticed that before. Were they always that cold, that steely?

Her hair was different too, not neat and conservative, tied back as it was at school, but hanging loose to her shoulders, almost wild, with stray bits flicking here and there.

And the clothes she wore were a far cry from the straight-laced outfits of a school office manager. She wore black leathers and cowboy boots.

The corners of her mouth turned up. I wouldn't go as far as saying it was a smile, as there was no warmth in it, not one bit. It was more of a smirk.

"You didn't think I was that stupid, did you?" Her voice was deeper, huskier than usual, and she was chewing gum.

I looked around, pretending I didn't know who she was speaking to. "Oh, you're talking to me," I said.

She snorted. "Funny guy. You thought I wouldn't twig that the cops were coming. Well, how did that work out?"

I would've liked to have come back with a joke, but that horrible throbbing in my head was only getting worse. "What happened?"

"They chucked you into the water," said Grandad. "There was a speedboat waiting. Clever trick. The police turned up a minute later. They never even saw where you went."

Mrs Cravat leant closer and blew a giant gum bubble in my face. It grew and grew and then it popped. "No one knows where you are." She laughed. I could hear Fred and Ginger chuckling in the background too. "Thanks though, for getting my diamonds back for me." She gazed up at the tribal mask, which was dangling from a pole above us, wafting gently in the breeze.

Grandad made a flapping motion. "Those Mumbari guys, they really are mad now. They've all come out again. 'Where are we?' they say. 'Where have they taken us?' I have tried to explain. They just want to go home." He turned and shouted, "Keep your heads, eh, boys!" Even though they didn't all have heads.

"What is this place?" I croaked.

"It's the 'Mammoth'," chipped in Sian. "One of those humungous cranes that sits on the banks of the Clyde."

"Very good, someone's been paying attention in class," said Mrs Cravat. "It's a giant cantilever crane to be exact, one of the last ones." She began strutting around, as if conducting a tour. "You know, I bought this thing for a pittance. My plan was to open it up as a tourist attraction. Fifty thousand fake visitors were going to pass through here every year."

"*Fake* visitors?" said Sian.

"Another one of her money-laundering businesses," I said. "She takes the hard cash she gets for selling the smuggled diamonds and puts it through one of her fake businesses. In this case, it would look like visitors were paying cash to come and see the crane. She puts it in a bank, and the money seems legitimate again."

"Wow!" said Sian. "That's fifty thousand people at, what, five pounds a head?"

"Seven pounds," said Mrs Cravat.

"Hmm…three hundred and fifty grand a year." Sian puffed her cheeks out. "That's a lot of laundry."

"Exactly," said Mrs Cravat. "You're quite the sleuth, aren't you, Mr Patel? And you, Ms Hanlon, quite the budding reporter. Well, thanks to you two and your meddling, all this is never going to happen." She poked a rusted piece of metal with her foot. It spun off the edge, into the darkness below. "Just as well, really. I mean, look at this place. It's a health and safety nightmare. In fact, the whole thing is on the point of falling down." She cupped her hands to her mouth and whispered, with a gleeful smirk, "There's a huge gas main underneath. It could blow at any moment. One spark, and…

"WHOOF!"

Mrs Cravat pointed out a bright orange glow in the skyline to the south. "See that? That's *Big A Printers* back in Pollockshields. That was my main money-laundering operation. It was part legit as well, to be fair, as we did the odd bit of printing work that came our way, just for appearances sake. Not that I could really be bothered. How did you link *Big A* to the murders, by the way?"

"I noticed that *Big A Printers* did equally bad work for the school and for *Duke's Laundry*."

"Shame, because of you it had to go. I'm good at starting fires, me. On the bright side, it was a brilliant diversion. Most of the emergency services in Glasgow are at the scene. Oh, and that includes your friends, Mr Patel. They all think that's where we took you. Like I said, no one knows you are here. Which means I can do what I want with you. And that's exactly what I'm going to do." She leaned even closer. I could smell the sweet bubblegum flavour on her breath, tinged with cigarette smoke and coffee. "A nice little explosion should do the trick."

CHAPTER 35

The Gangster Pancake

"You can't escape," I said to Mrs Cravat. "They know you're responsible for all this. They'll track you down."

"Na!" she said, with a self-satisfied grin. "I've got my cash, got my diamonds..." She patted a bulge in her jacket pocket. "Also got a private jet ready to whisk me off. By tomorrow morning I'll be in Brazil. They'll never get me. Of course, my boss won't be very happy. This was a nice little earner for him too, and you ruined it."

"Your boss?" I asked. "You have a boss?"

She shrugged. "Everyone has a boss, even in my business. He's a very important guy. He underwrote the whole thing. Dangerous too. But there are places in the world that even he can't reach, and that's where I'm going." She pushed herself up so she was sitting on top of a metal cabinet, swinging her legs. "So, how did you know it was me?"

"Yeah," said Grandad. "I want to know that too, because for the life of me I cannot work it out."

"A lot of things really," I said. "I kept thinking about what linked Morrison to the school. I mean, what brought him there. Then I checked out **Big A Printers** online.

Companies House have your name listed as company director. You wear a beaded African necklace and you have a huge African mask on your office wall – the only evidence I've ever seen of our supposed twin school in Africa."

Sian gasped and pointed a finger at Mrs Cravat. At least, she would have if she'd been able to move a finger. She couldn't even get it past her ear. "You! *You're* the person Morrison met on the Squinty Bridge."

"That's right," I said. "That's what you were about to tell me in the smoothie bar before Fred and Ginger kidnapped you."

"Yes, and don't think you weren't noticed, dear," Mrs Cravat said to her. "I saw you too that day on the bridge. Why else do you think I kidnapped you?"

"Morrison came to threaten you and demand more money," I said. "You killed Morrison with the wooden stave that goes with the mask. And then you called your business partner, Maw Cleggan, who sent over her two pals to help shift the body. Unfortunately, my mum found the body before they had a chance."

"But that wasn't the biggest clue," I said. "There was Big Davie. He died before he could report what we'd found on the CCTV. I checked the school handbook, the one printed by *Big A*. It said:

All incidents of a criminal nature are
to be reported through the school office.

That's when I worked out, he *didn't* go and shift the grand piano first, like he said he was going to do. He must have changed his mind. He must have thought better of it, given that there was a dead body and all. He came and spoke to you first, the school office manager."

She laughed and folded her arms. "You really do have it all worked out, don't you? Yes, poor Davie. He came to me, told me he'd found some evidence that the body was really there. Although he never mentioned the CCTV. I didn't work that one out until later."

"The following morning to be exact," I said. "That's when you sent Fred and Ginger back to Davie's office. At lunchtime, when you knew it would be quiet. As for Maw Cleggan..." I gazed out at the two figures shifting in the darkness, and raised my voice. "Did you two know Mrs Cravat killed your boss?"

The two figures became very still. I could sense their shock.

"Yes, it was Mrs Cravat who put her in the tumble dryer, not me."

"Oh, call me Julie, please." Mrs Cravat laughed, and jumped down off the cabinet. "I was wondering when this would come up."

Fred and Ginger, on the other side of the walkway, both stepped closer. For a second their faces appeared in the light from the streets. Fred's face was horrified, Ginger's was just plain horrifying.

"You... YOU killed Maw?" stuttered Fred.

Mrs Cravat opened out her hands and jiggled her fingers about. "Ta-daa! It was me."

Ginger whimpered. "Maw was like a... well, like a maw to us."

"Yes, I know, boo-hoo, it's all very sad," said Mrs Cravat. "She started questioning my methods, and she threatened to report me to the big boss. She had to go."

Fred's face changed from shocked to angry, to downright murderous. "Come on, Ginger, let's do her!" Ginger nodded, then his face curled into a snarl. He delved into his boiler suit and pulled out a crowbar. The two men leapt forward, one after the other, over the low railings and across the gap between the walkways.

Mrs Cravat was totally unruffled by this. She didn't even drop her smirk. She simply turned and pulled a lever.

With a loud whirring noise, a hulking shadow behind her came to life. It shunted forward, just as Fred and Ginger were crossing in front of it.

"Uh, what?" was all Fred had time to say, as the moving machinery bumped into him, swept him off his feet and sent him flying over the edge.

"AAAAAHHH!"

Ginger followed closely behind.

"UH... AAAHHHH!"

The two men barely had time to wrap their arms round each other's necks as they fell.

Seconds later, I heard a **CRUMP** ... **CRUMP** below us.

"Anyone fancy a gangster pancake?" joked Grandad.

Mrs Cravat pulled the lever again. The machinery stopped whirring. Then she grinned at me. "The crane's hoist mechanism still works, which is terribly useful at times like this."

"STOP THIS!" came another voice from the other end of the crane. This time even Mrs Cravat looked surprised. Another figure stepped out of the shadows, wielding something cold, gleaming and metallic.

The Top-Secret Grandad

A set of piercing brown eyes appeared from under a wide-brimmed fedora. The man's accent was familiar: Portuguese. Valente stepped into the light. He was clutching a pair of scissors.

"I represent the Global Diamond Federation."

"Aw, not this guy again!" said Grandad.

"I expect you're a bit peeved that I nicked all your diamonds," said Mrs Cravat.

"I am here to negotiate." Valente's gaze then shifted to me. "But you can't kill this boy ..."

I was about to breathe a sigh of relief. Maybe this guy wasn't as bad as I thought. Maybe he was going to rescue us. "At least," he continued, "not until I have finished his hair; it's a disaster."

"Seriously?" said Sian.

He held up his scissors and started snipping them. "Yes, seriously." He smiled at Mrs Cravat. A broad, white-toothed smile. "Don't worry, we can do a deal on the diamonds."

"Oh, this is getting tiresome," said Mrs Cravat. "Look, I'm not really in the deal-doing business."

She whipped out a long thin tube from inside her leather jacket. She took a deep breath and blew into it, aiming at Valente.

A lightning fast projectile whizzed past my head.

"Ow!" Valente clutched his neck. "What was that?"

"African blow-pipe," replied Mrs Cravat. "Very useful weapon. I picked it up on one of my many trips to Africa."

"But... but..." Valente stared at her for a second, then at me. He looked sad, snipped his scissors a few more times, then his eyes rolled and he fell sideways, off the walkway grill and into the darkness.

CRUMP

"She is the flippin' angel of death, this one," said Grandad.

Mrs Cravat clapped her palms together like a teacher at the end of a satisfactory lesson. "I'm pleased that's that taken care of."

"Oh, wait," said Grandad. Valente's dark glasses had landed on the grill nearby. Now they were glowing a ghostly green. Grandad snatched them up, flipped them open and slid them on. "At last, a pair of shades. This is perfect!" He turned to me and opened out his hands.

"Look at me, boy.
Top-secret Grandad!"

"I'm going to leave you two lovebirds to your doom," said Mrs Cravat. "Here, watch this…" She placed what looked like a clock radio with a red LED display on top of the metal cabinet she'd been sitting on. It was wrapped in duct tape and connected to a wire, which ran down below the walkway, presumably all the way to the bottom of the crane. She footered with the buttons for a second, then set the red clock numbers to 10:00. She popped up a red button on the top, and then turned and grinned at us. A huge, smug grin that said she'd won and she was in control. "A nice little countdown," she said. "Ten minutes. And then, BOOM! You, Mr Patel, and you, Ms Hanlon, will be no longer be thorns in my side. By the time they sift through the wreckage and figure out what happened, I'll be well on my way."

She tapped one of the buttons, which immediately began the clock's countdown:

09:59
09:58

Mrs Cravat gave one final laugh, before dashing across the walkway and disappearing down a ladder.

CHAPTER 37

The Button Dilemma

"Well," said Sian, tugging on the ropes tying us to the railing, "looks like I'm not getting any Christmas presents this year."

"Grandad!" I said. "Do something!"

"Grandad?" she asked. What's this, an imaginary relative?"

"You may as well tell her, boy," said Grandad. "Not that she'll believe you."

"Uh," I sighed, and collected myself. But how was I supposed to explain to Sian that the ghost of my dead grandad was haunting me. And, indeed, was helping me investigate crimes. It wasn't going to be easy. Especially as we only had ten minutes to live. "My grandad's ghost. Only I can see it. He follows me around everywhere."

"Oh," said Sian. "that's... er..."

"Rubbish!" said Grandad. "You make me sound like a Labrador. I do not just follow you around. Why don't you tell her how many times I have saved your skin?"

"OK, OK," I said. "He is quite useful sometimes. Also quite ANNOYING."

"RR-IIIGHT," said Sian, staring at me like my head was spinning round. "A ghostly grandfather. That's new."

"Show some respect for your elders, boy," said Grandad.

"I can prove it," I said. "Look."

"I hope you can be quick about it," said Sian, trying to wriggle her wrist out of a knot and failing. "Cos if we hang about much longer, pretty soon we'll be joining him."

"She's right, boy," said Grandad. "We have to think fast!"

09:01

"Grandad, blow in her ear."

Grandad bent down, took a breath and then puffed in her right ear, like a strong gust of wind blowing up from nowhere. Sian's hair flew sideways for a moment. Then the gust died away.

"Wo! That's interesting," she said.

"Don't worry, I won't ask him to sneeze on you."

"That's very kind of you," said Sian, "but I don't believe in ghosts. At least for the next ten minutes. After that I'm likely to become one myself."

"I am afraid you might, young lady," said Grandad, "because I cannot stop this clock."

"Grandad, you HAVE TO hit that button! Our lives depend on it," I said.

Sian began rubbing her wrist along the rusted edge of the railing. "If I can just cut through the rope... I mean, it will take a while. Probably too long. But it's worth a go."

Grandad shrugged, and turned to try the button. He strained, but nothing happened. "I cannot move it, boy,

I am sorry, it's too stiff and takes too much energy. Even a big juicy sneeze won't press that button down."

It was no good. Both Sian and me were tied up tight by the wrists, and Grandad was limited to passing various types of wind. I didn't see any way we could press that button. I didn't see any way out of this one at all.

CHAPTER 38

The Countdown Song

"Wait a minute," said Grandad. "I'm forgetting my friends."

"What friends?" I asked.

"What? Friends?" said Sian, frantically sawing the rope against the rusty edge of the railing.

"My *friends*," said Grandad, pointing up at the mask, which was still swinging from the pole in the breeze.

"Oh, *those* friends," I said.

"Here, I'll show you." Grandad blinked. Suddenly the platform was alive with the ghosts of the Mumbari, who were all standing about, yelling.

"Guys! Guys, guys!" called Grandad. "Do you think for one minute we could have a little quiet? We need to help my grandson and his girlfriend."

The men's ghastly faces all twisted towards me. I gave them a pained smile. "She's not my girlfriend."

"Who? What?" said Sian.

"I promise you guys," said Grandad. "If you help us this one last time, my grandson there will get you and your mask home where you belong."

"What's going on?" asked Sian.

I rubbed my head, trying to work out how I could possibly begin to explain, that we were negotiating for help with a tribe of African ghosts. "Eh... Doesn't matter."

The ghosts grunted, groaned and wailed in approval, and some of them nodded too, except for one, who didn't have a head. He just wiggled his neck back and forward.

"I think we can press that button down and stop the clock," said Grandad. "But we will all have to work together, pool all our energy into one." He pointed out a rusted old wrench lying on the walkway. "Look, there. Why don't we use that?"

The ghostly tribesmen grunted and moaned again, except for the one without the head, who just whistled air through the hole in his neck.

"Come on, then!" Grandad knelt down and tried grasping hold of the wrench. His hand wouldn't budge it. One of the tribesmen knelt down and joined him, then another, and another. One by one they knelt down until they were all clutching at the wrench.

Spectral veins bulged in Grandad's temples.

"HEAVE!"

Every one of them was straining, but the wrench still wouldn't move.

Then, one of them started singing. It was one of those African tribal songs. One by one the men picked up the melody, harmonizing with each other, singing as one. Even the one without a head could carry a tune.

Just as I was beginning to give up hope the impossible happened. The wrench moved.

First, a grudging centimetre. Then, a hopeful inch, and then, a joyful and magical foot into the air.

"YESSSS!" I cried.

"OHHHH!" cried Sian.

"We're doing it! We're doing it!" yelled Grandad.

"So... there really is a ghost," said Sian.

"Oh, yes," I said.

"Careful! Careful lads!" said Grandad, as he and his chanting friends stepped slowly towards the countdown clock. A clock that was creeping slowly but surely towards zero.

03:32

Slowly, step-by-step, and inch-by-inch, until finally the spanner was poised right above the red button.

"OK, lads, slowly, let it down," said Grandad.

Still chanting, the group lowered the wrench down on top of the button.

02:13

And there it stopped, resting on top of it. For a heart-stopping moment I thought it wasn't going any further, that the wrench wasn't heavy enough, or the button was stuck.

01:30

"Push it down! Down!" cried Grandad.

The entire team screwed their faces up, even the one who only had half a face, as they pushed down on the wrench.

"Come on! Come on!" I yelled.

They pushed and pushed, until at last the button jolted down, and the wrench tumbled off the edge and fell away. But it was OK, because the clock had stopped.

0:18

"YESSSSS!" cried Grandad, leading his fellow ghosts in celebration. There were high-fives all round, even for the ghost with no hands – he used his feet instead.

"Right," said Sian, shocked. "So, ghosts exist... That's going to take a while to sink in."

"Now we just need to get free of these ropes," I said.

"And catch Mrs Cravat," she added.

"If we're lucky, we might just be in the nick of time."

I sat back, laughing, watching the African ghost men dance in celebration around the walkway. Grandad joined in at the back. "I LOVE these guys!" he said, and high-fived the man with no head.

CHAPTER 39

The Terminal Swoop

The precinct outside Glasgow airport thronged with people. Judging by all the loud shirts on display and the sun-tanned limbs, a couple of tourist planes must have just landed. Our taxi screeched to a halt outside. We'd flagged down a people carrier because it was bigger, and we had a lot of people in tow, or should I say ex-people. I slid the door open, and Sian dumped a five-pound note and a lolly in the taxi driver's hand.

He looked grateful. If only he knew he'd just given a lift to about two dozen ghosts.

Carrying the mask under my arm, I led the others into the terminal building, only to find the police were already there. They'd just arrived. A small army of officers was streaming through another entrance. I'd managed to phone DI Graves after we escaped from the crane.

I spotted Graves leading a pack of armed officers. She beckoned us over to her. "You two! Come on!"

They were moving fast, creating a lot of noise and excitement among the crowd of travellers checking in.

We ran straight through the passport controls, then down a long corridor. Before we knew it, we were running out onto the tarmac. Patrol cars sped across the far end of the runway, sirens blaring, heading for a private plane that was taxiing for take-off.

"That must be her," said Sian.

"It's too late," I heard Graves say. "The cars are too far away to stop her, and so are we."

"PAH!" said Grandad, and he looked around at the gawping faces, (or, in some cases, gawping neck-holes), of his fellow ghosts. "That's the woman who stole your mask." The African ghosts howled. "Let's see what happens when ghosts really do get into the machine."

The others nodded gleefully, and then Grandad led them floating towards the plane.

"CH-AAAAARGGE!!"

The plane turned sharply and revved its engines. Once the pilot hit the thruster and sped down the runway we'd have no chance of catching up.

One by one, Grandad and the other ghosts twisted up into the air and dive-bombed into the engines. Both engines roared, then made a wheezing, cranking noise, before spluttering out.

The police cars swooped in, screeching to a halt in front of the plane. Armed officers gathered all around. Eventually, the door opened and a figure stepped out, blonde and wearing black leathers. Her face was white.

DI Graves strode towards her. "Mrs Cravat, you're under arrest."

Mrs Cravat glared over at me, as I leant on Sian's shoulder trying to catch my breath. She shook her head and spat, "Kids!"

Grandad and his posse of tribesmen spewed out the back of the engine and landed on the tarmac in an invisible heap. Grandad sat up, nursing his head. "Well, that is definitely the last time I am doing that."

CHAPTER 40

The Final Rammy

The police car pulled away, carrying in the back seat an extremely angry and extremely handcuffed Mrs Cravat.

"Don't worry," Grandad called after her, "JEWEL be out in twenty years." He turned to me and nodded. "Get it? *Jewel?*"

I groaned.

DI Graves appeared at my shoulder. She seemed slightly less grim than usual, now that the mystery had been solved and the criminal captured. "Well done, Jay Patel," she said. "But, I really mean this in the nicest possible way – I NEVER want to see you again."

"Huh! Suits us," said Grandad.

Constable McBurnie appeared, panting and covered in dirt and twigs and bits of spider web. He was holding a wooden club in front of him. When I'd told DI Graves about the stave earlier that day, over the phone, she'd sent McBurnie off to the country park to search for it. "Here it is, that bit of wood you made me look for."

"The murder weapon? Thank you." Graves snatched it off him. With the slightest hint of a smile, and I mean the slightest – an eagle with a magnifying glass might have missed it – she turned and melted into the crowd of police officers.

McBurnie stared round at the scene. "Ach! Did I miss ANOTHER rammy?"

"'Fraid so," I replied.

"AAAAH!"

He plucked the police hat from his head and tossed it away. "That's it, I quit!"

"You quit? Why?"

"Aye. Being a polis is nothing like I thought it would be. I heard there's a janitor's job going at your school. That seems to be where all the action is. I might put in for that." He marched off.

"So," said Sian, "you're living with a ghost, one that only you can see. What's that like, I wonder?" She drummed her fingers on her chin, then snapped them together. "That's it! I'm going to do a feature on you, Jay Patel. It'll be my next big story. I'm going to make you FAMOUS." She circled me, making a square with her fingers, sizing me up for the headline shot. "How do you feel about THAT?"

"How do I feel? Hmm…" I shared a quick glance with Grandad, then I pretended to notice something in the distance. "Ooh, what's that over there, behind the plane? That could be important…"

"What?" She turned away.

I picked up the mask and legged it. Now it was my turn to merge into the background, this time for good. Once a case is solved, no good detective worth his salt sticks around.

CHAPTER 41

The White Envelope

Back home, Mum and Granny hadn't even noticed I was out. I planted the mask down in the hall, and listened at Mum's door. Whale noises were playing, which meant she was asleep. How whale noises were meant to help anyone get to sleep was beyond me. It sounded like polar bears constantly throwing up.

Granny was snoring in front of the telly while a zombie movie was playing. They were her favourite for some reason. If only she knew the dead really could return from the grave, I thought. She was still wearing her DIY goggles. I carefully picked them off and placed them on a side table.

Grandad slung his coat on a hook, along with his hat. He peeled off his sunglasses, folded them up and stuck them in his pocket.

I flopped onto the bed, too exhausted to even undress or clear off the mess. "Night, Grandad."

"Night, Jayesh." He plonked his ghostly buttocks down on my bedroom chair, among a pile of papers. "You deserve a good night's sleep."

He might have been annoying sometimes, but I had to admit, there was something quite nice and comforting knowing he'd be there all night, watching over me.

Maybe that's why I slept like a log. When I woke, he was still there, resting his elbows on his knees. "What would you like?" he asked. "The good news or the bad news?"

I yawned and sat up. "Is there any middle-ish news you can give me instead?"

"OK," he sighed. "The bad news is, the African lads, they do not wish to return home any more."

"Eh?"

"Look, see." He blinked then flung open the bedroom door. Granny had her workbench set up in the hall, and was planing the edges off some wood. The Mumbari were leaning over, checking out her work, admiring the smoothness of her finish, and nodding and grunting in approval, even the ones with no heads. "They are quite taken with her. They say she is a goddess. I can hardly disagree with them. I mean, look at her: my girl." Granny had just bent over, her bandy legs splayed out, to pick up a T-square.

I swiped my hand. "They're going home, and that's that!"

"WHIT?" cried Granny.

"Nothing, Granny," I said.

"I'll make your porridge, laddie." She whisked off her goggles and gloves and scurried into the kitchen. The Mumbari trailed after her, excited. They'd never seen porridge before. I hoped they wouldn't be disappointed.

"So, what's the good news?" I asked.

"Well, I think I have figured out why I am here," said Grandad.

"You have?"

"Oh, yes. Definitely. I am here to help you find your father again."

I nodded. "Good, because I really need your help, Grandad."

He gave me a ghostly grin, then rolled up his sleeves and stepped into the middle of my bedroom, gazing purposefully at the maps and newspaper cuttings, and all the evidence I'd gathered over the last nine months. "Come on, then," he said. "What are you waiting for? An invitation?"

As I walked into the hall, a white envelope dropped through the letterbox. I stared at it for a moment, then stared at Grandad. It was a funny coincidence, coming right at that moment. I wasn't altogether sure I believed in coincidence any more, not after all the things that had happened to me lately.

I picked it up. The envelope was addressed to me and Mum, the two of us.

Mrs K Patel & Master J Patel

We walked back into my bedroom, where I sat down on the bed, thumbed the envelope open, and slid out a folded piece of paper.

"Well?" Grandad asked. "What is it?"

"An invitation."

Mrs K Patel & Master J Patel

CONGRATULATIONS!!!

YOU HAVE WON A FABULOUS
WEEKEND BREAK AT A LUXURY
COUNTRY HOUSE HOTEL!

WE LOOK FORWARD
TO WELCOMING YOU AT
THE BRIGHTBURGH MANOR.

TO BE CONTINUED...

TOP-SECRET GRANDAD and me

Jay Patel and his ghost grandad will be back soon with a brand new case to solve in:

DEATH By SOUP

INCIDENT REPORT:
Jay and his mum have won a weekend break at a fancy hotel in the countryside. But the holiday turns foul when one of the guests mysteriously drops dead over dinner...
Can Jay and Grandad solve the case before the killer strikes again?

CRIME:
Murder

CAUSE OF DEATH:
Chicken noodle soup

SUSPECTS:
- Timothy Shand (hotel manager)
- Lord Brightburgh (VERY posh)
- Vera Hackenbottom (a guest)
- The chef

DETECTIVES:
Top-Secret Grandad and Me

Also by David MacPhail

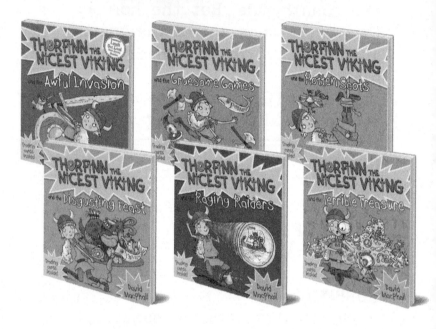

Prepare yourself for the wrath of the Norsemen! That is, if you don't mind and it's not too inconvenient...

Thorfinn, The Nicest Viking is a funny and fearsome new series for young readers who love *Horrid Henry* and *Diary of a Wimpy Kid*, set in a world where manners mean nothing and politeness is pointless!

 Also available as eBooks

DiscoverKelpies.co.uk

If you loved Jay and Grandad, try these next!

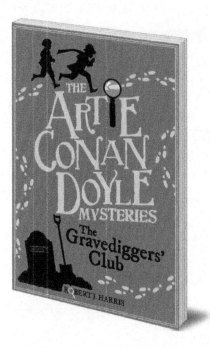

Book 1 in The Artie Conan Doyle Mysteries

A ghostly lady in grey. The paw prints of a gigantic hound. This case can only be solved by the world's greatest detective.

No, not Sherlock Holmes! Meet boy-detective Artie Conan Doyle, the real brains behind Sherlock. With the help of best friend Ham, Artie discovers the secrets of the spooky Gravediggers' Club. Can Artie solve the mystery – or will his first case be his last?

 Also available as an eBook

DiscoverKelpies.co.uk

Slugboy Saves the World

Thanks to an unfortunately tasty-looking radioactive garden slug, eleven-year-old Murdo McLeod is now the world's worst superhero.

In a Scotland full of awesome superheroes, Slugboy has a lot to prove. Can he use his not-so-super and oh-so-gross abilities to save the world? Let's hope he doesn't slip up...

DiscoverKelpies.co.uk